Too Sweet

GRACE TURNER

contents

To any woman who has ever loved another woman.
Whether silently or out loud.

author's note

This book is intended for adults and contains sexually explicit situations. It's really just a spicy, romantic good time. However, it does include one of the characters being publicly "outed." Although the fallout is not negative, and everyone is very accepting.

If you have any questions about the content of this book, please feel free to email me at graceturnerauthor@gmail.com or send me a message @graceturnerauthor on Instagram.

Happy reading!!

one
. . .

Evin

I STABBED and stabbed and *stabbed* the backspace button. I felt like the shittiest writer in the world.

My creativity was gone, as was everything I'd ever learned about storytelling. Leaning back in my desk chair, I looked up from my laptop screen to the window in front of me. The sun was cresting the horizon, and the park beneath my apartment was crowded with people enjoying the last of the spring weather. Summer was right around the corner, and in Texas, it came swiftly and without mercy.

I unclipped my hair and massaged my scalp. I longed to be out there with them, but I'd promised myself I would have at least a thousand words done before I got up from my chair.

I had ten words. Ten, then I'd deleted them all, anyway.

A little independent publishing company that was interested in expanding into the mystery and thriller genres had taken a chance on my last book. Now, they were expecting me to write another one.

They'd been flexible with the timeline since they knew I still had a full-time job as a virtual assistant, but it had to happen eventually. And I was off to the shittiest start imaginable.

The attention of a publisher meant a lot. It meant I didn't have to front the money to publish the book myself or oversee all the marketing, editing, and everything in between.

It meant a lot, especially right now when it felt like I was working hard yet not really going anywhere. My dream of being a full-time author felt like it was farther away every day.

Ready to give up for the night and start fresh the next day, I walked the few feet to my fridge and peered inside. I hadn't been grocery shopping recently, so I wasn't sure what I thought I was going to find. I shut the fridge and turned around to lean against it. Peering around my studio, I decided that I wasn't going to stay cooped up in my little six-hundred-foot box any longer.

Maybe my writing muse would find me again outside my four walls.

I walked back to my little bedroom corner and straightened my sheets before I grabbed my phone from my desk directly across from it. My best friend, Aiden, who I was about to invite to dinner, was already calling me.

"Hey, I was just about to call you. Do you want—"

"Have you seen it?" he asked quickly.

"Umm..." I stuttered. "I don't think so, but I also have no idea what you're talking about, so I can't be sure."

He sighed, and there was some shuffling on the other end of the line. I leaned my hip against the edge of my desk and continued my longing stare out the window.

"Google Lucy Lowe interview. It's the one she did recently for her new movie."

"You want me to Google Lucy Lowe?"

"Yes, that's exactly what I want you to do, and you need to do it right this second."

I groaned and fell back into my desk chair. I'd paid extra for one that was super comfy and large, but I still hated it at that moment. It only reminded me of how poorly writing was going.

"That groan was not a response. Are you doing it? I need to hear typing."

"Oh my gosh, yes, Aiden. I'm typing furiously. Give me a second," I said. I put him on speakerphone and set the phone next to my laptop. I typed in exactly what he told me—"*Lucy Lowe interview*"—and hit enter. So many videos popped up.

"Can you clarify why I'm doing this?" I asked as I scrolled.

There was more commotion in the background, and he mumbled a curse. Aiden was a curator at a luxury home furnishing store, and I was guessing he'd stepped into the back room to call me. I'd only visited him there once, but you couldn't walk through that room without running into or tripping over something.

"I promise you'll know it when you see it. She's wearing a blue jumpsuit in the interview. I probably should have told you to look up her name and yours, but…"

He said that at the same time I clicked on the interview, and the video automatically started playing.

"What?" I croaked out. "Why would I search our names together? Me and Lucy Lowe? She is one of the most famous people in the world, and I am—well, I'm not."

Aiden chuckled. "The degrees of separation are about to become far fewer. Just watch. Are you watching?"

"Yes, I'm watching."

I folded my hands in my lap and sat back in my chair. Lucy Lowe was beautiful. Long dark hair and striking green eyes, I understood why some people were crazy obsessed with her. I wasn't one of those people, but you couldn't look at her and not appreciate her beauty.

But it wasn't just her appearance, it was how she held herself, too, that made her so irresistibly enigmatic. She was so confident and sure of herself, it was hard not to watch when she was on the screen.

"*So, in this movie, you play a struggling writer with a penchant for collecting books. Have you read anything recently you've really loved?*" the interviewer asked.

"This is the part!" Aiden suddenly shouted through the phone. So engrossed in the video, I'd honestly forgotten he was still there.

I straightened and sat forward.

"*Yes, I actually have!*" Lucy exclaimed and motioned to someone off-camera. "*Can you grab the book that's in my bag? Yes, it should be over there.*" A few seconds later, a random person walked on screen and handed her a book. She gave him a sincere smile and thanked him quickly.

"*If you've never read Evin Morgan, you are truly missing out.*"

My breath caught in my throat, and I stabbed the space bar on my laptop.

"Evin? Wait, what just happened?"

My jaw dropped open, and I fumbled for my next words. I could hardly believe it when I said them. "She just...she just said my name."

"She did! Keep watching. It gets better."

"Aiden, I—" I stuttered out, still unable to put together a coherent thought, let alone an actual sentence.

"Evin!" Aiden chastised, and I pressed play.

"*This is her most recent book, and I'm not even done yet,*" Lucy said, holding up my most recent release. "*But it's likely going to be my favorite. She is just the best storyteller, and I never guess the twist. If you like thrillers, you have to read her books.*"

"*With a review like that, I just might,*" the interviewer said. She changed the topic after that, but Lucy sat with my book in her lap the rest of the interview, clutching it like it was her most prized possession.

"I'm going to give you a moment to process," Aiden said, and it wasn't just a moment. It was several minutes later that I finally wrapped my head around what I'd just heard.

Lucy Lowe, one of the most famous people on the planet, just promoted my book in an interview that would be posted everywhere. A few sentences, and she'd possibly changed my life forever.

"Now that you've had a second, go look at your social media."

With shaking hands, I picked up my phone and opened the first app I saw. I blinked a few times and squinted at the notifications and numbers I saw. I'd turned my phone on silent when I'd started writing—or attempted to start writing—so I hadn't received notifications about the hundreds of new comments or followers.

And every second I had the app open, another one popped up. A new follower saying they'd just downloaded the book or someone else saying they were going to binge-read it that night.

"What the fuck?" I muttered, scrolling through the endless stream of excitement.

A new text from my editor popped up at the top of my screen with a million exclamation points and a ton of emojis. This coming from the woman who sent me "looks great" after reading what she claimed was my best work.

"This is your big break, Evin. This could be it," Aiden said, and I opened my account listing all my book sales. It didn't necessarily update in real-time, but it was somewhat accurate.

In the last hour, I'd sold more books than I had in the last three months combined.

"I—I—how did she even find me? My books aren't physically in any major bookstores yet. Maybe an indie bookstore, but that—"

"It doesn't matter!" Aiden whisper-shouted. "Sorry, I'm almost done at work, then I'm coming over and we're celebrating. Because it doesn't matter how she found you. You're an amazing writer, an amazing freaking person, and you deserve all the success that's about to come your way. So, stop questioning it, and be happy! I've gotta go, but I'll bring food and wine. I'll be there in thirty minutes."

He hung up, and tears gathered in my eyes. Turning back to my computer, I restarted the video and watched it a few more times to make sure I wasn't hallucinating.

Thankfully, I wasn't, and I knew my life would never be the same.

two

. . .

Lucy

"BYE, Ms. Lowe, I'll see you next week," Ricardo called as he turned left toward the front door, and I headed to the kitchen at the back of the house.

"Bye, Ricky. Thanks so much."

When I was at home, which was less and less often as of late, Ricardo was my trainer. Or more like my workout buddy. I genuinely enjoyed his company and loved our workouts when they happened, but it was also kind of sad that I had to pay someone to come spend time with me.

I didn't have a lot of friends in LA. Actually, I didn't have *any* friends. Several years in the city, and all I had to show for it was a nice, very empty house. A house that was less reminiscent of the modern homes surrounding it and more like the little country home I wanted and would have had if I'd stayed in Oklahoma.

My family was still back in Oklahoma in the house I'd grown up in. I'd paid off their mortgage after my first big movie and built a gate around their property with security cameras. I missed it every day. I missed everything about it—the wide-open space, slower way of life, my parents, and my older brother.

But every day I got to live most people's dream and did what I loved.

Thankfully, today was a slower day. I'd rolled out of bed at nine that morning and worked out for an hour. The rest of my plans included reading and shutting out the rest of the world. It was much needed before we continued our long press tour for my newest movie.

I pulled open the fridge and grabbed the ingredients to make my usual post-workout smoothie. Laying them all out on the counter, I retrieved a cutting board from one of the lower cabinets and a knife from the block when someone yelled my name from the front of the house.

I startled and almost cut myself as my manager, Madison, came around the corner. She looked up from her phone to see me standing in the middle of the kitchen, covered in sweat and wielding a large knife.

"You scared the shit out of me. I almost cut myself," I said.

Her eyes widened, and she shrugged, cringing apologetically. "Sorry, you said you wanted me to announce myself."

I shook my head and waved her off as I went back to the fruit in front of me. Madison had been my manager for years, and we'd formed a respectful, strictly professional relationship. I was thankful for her every day. She kept my life in order.

"We need to go over your schedule for the next few weeks," Madison said, rounding the butcher block island and slipping into one of the barstools across from me.

I nodded, and she looked up from her phone and notebook long enough to look incredulously at the fruit I'd already cut and was adding to the blender.

"Lucy, honey, I've told you that I'll hire you a chef. You have the money to pay someone to do this for you," she said. It was the same argument we had about everything. Having money meant I never had to lift a finger again, but I wasn't interested. I swore she'd hire someone to wipe my ass if I asked.

She knew what I'd say, so instead of responding, I just gave her the same look I always did. She raised her hands in mock surrender and began reciting my very hectic, very busy schedule for the next few months. *Months* of insanity.

There were a few days when I didn't have an appearance or other commitment scheduled, but not enough to amount to any real time off. Two days in the Midwest that I could spend with my family and a few on the East Coast.

I started blending my smoothie once she was finally finished.

"Oh, and that interview you did a few days ago," Madison began as I poured the contents into my favorite cup. "The one where you talked about Evin Morgan's book? They posted it, and it's gotten some really great feedback. I looked at the author's account, and she's gained a few thousand new followers just in the past twenty-four hours."

I dumped the blender and cutting board in the sink to deal with later as I whipped back around to Madison. "No way?"

She nodded and showed me her phone screen. Sure enough, Evin had thousands of followers. I wasn't sure how many she'd had before, but I was impressed.

"All because of my interview?"

"Yup," she said, popping the "p." "You're influential. What you say makes an impact."

I took a sip of my smoothie and couldn't contain my smile. I didn't know much of Evin—she was pretty private on social media—but I knew she was a hell of a writer. She had a way of constructing a story that put you in the action and kept you on the edge of your seat. She deserved all the notoriety. She should have been a bestseller.

"She even reposted a clip of the interview and tagged you in it." Madison slid her phone across the counter to me. Evin thanked me for reading and everyone for all their support. She said something like this was life-changing for her, and she was forever grateful.

"I'm so excited for her. She really is so good," I said, sliding the phone back.

"Her sales have to be off the charts. Just one interview did all that," Madison muttered, back to typing away. I'd long ago deleted all social media apps from my phone. I was being inundated with messages—both good and bad—and the pressure of keeping up with it made me anxious.

So, one of the things I *had* spent money on was hiring a social media manager. Bailey posted for me a few times a week, and I promised to send her photos she could use whenever I could. Because she was the only one who touched my socials, I had no idea any of this had happened. But I wanted to do more.

"So, if I made a dedicated post, that would be even better, right?"

"A dedicated post to your almost one hundred million followers? Yes, that would make a huge difference." Immediately, I reached for my own phone sitting next to me. "But Lucy, that's not really your brand, and I'm not sure Bailey would—"

I shook my head and shot a quick text to Bailey about what I wanted to do. She responded within seconds that she loved the idea.

"She loves it," I told Madison, showing her the text exchange. "I'll take a cute little picture after I shower and post a review. I did that interview before I'd finished, so now I can tell people for certain it's amazing. Beginning to end."

three

. . .

Lucy

Two hours later, with a light face of makeup and no sweat in sight, I snapped a picture with all Evin Morgan's books. Because I owned all of them in both paperback and ebook formats.

I wrote up a review—although I didn't sound as eloquent as Evin—and with Bailey's help, posted it. I re-downloaded the app only for the day so I could see the feedback and watch Evin's numbers grow in real time.

In the first minute it was up, it already had ten thousand likes. I would never get over that. Bailey made sure to tag Evin in the post, and within half an hour, Evin's follower count was on the steady increase.

I was sitting on my bed, trying to find a new book to read, when Bailey texted me.

> Bailey: Evin sent you a DM if you want to look at it.

I'd met some of the greatest actors, musicians, producers, and directors of my lifetime, and worked with plenty of them, too.

But nothing compared to the giddy excitement I felt when I tapped open the message from Evin.

> **@evinmorganauthor:** I know you probably don't read your DMs, so you may never see this, but thank you so much for reading and supporting me! You've genuinely changed my life for the better. I don't know how you found my books, but this is just incredible. I'm going to stop now before I start gushing and embarrass myself. Just thank you, thank you!

There wasn't a second thought as I sat up and started typing a response.

> **@lucylowe:** Evin, you are so talented. I feel honored to have read your books. Please keep writing. I will continue to be your biggest fan!

> **@evinmorganauthor:** I'm sorry, I'm in shock that you responded. Give me a moment to process that you're my number one fan.

I laughed out loud and stood from my bed to walk out onto the patio. It was a beautiful view of rolling hills, littered with multi-million-dollar homes.

> **@lucylowe:** I'm absolutely your #1 fan! I could talk about your books all day, and I have so many questions for you. I found your first book at a little indie bookstore while doing a press tour for my last movie. I've been hooked ever since and anxiously await each book you publish.

> **@evinmorganauthor:** That's incredible! Only a few indie bookstores purchased a couple copies, so that's insane you actually found one. It's fate.

@lucylowe: Kismet :)

Looking out into the distance, I contemplated my next message. Almost everyone in my life would tell me that it's stupid and reckless and a bad idea, and it probably was, but I couldn't stop myself. I was talking to my favorite author, and I had the opportunity to discuss her books. I wasn't going to let that chance slip away.

@lucylowe: I know this might be weird, but I try to stay off social media. Can I give you my number, and maybe we could text? I have so many questions, and I'd love to discuss your work.

I pressed send and waited with bated breath, my phone in a death grip between my hands. The bubble appeared that she was typing, then it disappeared. It reappeared, then disappeared once more, and I was on the verge of tossing it down on one of the deck chairs and walking away when it vibrated with a new message.

@evinmorganauthor: When I woke up this morning, I never thought this is how my day would end up. But here we are! Feel free to text me any time. 972-654-2544

Quickly, I copied her number and added her as a new contact. A minute later, I was sending her a text and deleting all social media from my phone once again.

Evin responded, and I forgot about anything else I'd wanted to do that day.

four

...

Lucy

DROPPING onto my hotel room bed, I kicked my heels off and heard them thump to the ground.

I stared up at the white, coffered ceiling and blew out a deep breath. Twelve-plus hours of interviews and other press events, and all I wanted to do was sleep.

And possibly talk to Evin.

I flipped onto my stomach and retrieved my phone from my pocket.

> Evin Morgan: You have to watch it. That season 3 finale was…soul-crushing.

Smiling at my phone, I scrolled back through our recent text messages and reminded myself of our conversation. I hadn't had much time throughout the day to respond, so I'd missed her text from several hours ago.

My thumbs hovered over the keyboard, but my brain was so tired, I couldn't think of a response. But I still really wanted to talk to Evin.

We'd spent the past month forming a pretty strong friendship. The concept of which was so foreign to me, I'd almost forgotten what it felt like.

We texted often and talked on the phone a few times, and I was more captivated with Evin each and every time we spoke. Not in my wildest dreams did I ever think my favorite author would become my friend.

Yes, she was an amazing author, and we'd talked endlessly about her books. But she was also a really good, genuine person. She was kind and funny and...I really enjoyed getting to know her. Often, talking to her was the best part of my day.

Shaking my head to dislodge the thoughts, I didn't hesitate to press the video call button next to her name. The camera popped up, and I cringed at my appearance. My makeup had long worn off, showing off the dark circles under my eyes and the stress breakout I was sporting on my chin.

Evin answered quickly, except the camera was pointed toward the ceiling of whatever room she was in.

"Hi, one second, I just got out of the shower," Evin called from somewhere else in what I assumed was her bathroom. Especially with the way her voice echoed.

"No problem, if you want to call me back—" I began, but she cut me off quickly.

"No, no. Just two seconds."

She cursed under her breath, and I smiled to myself. Dragging my hand through my hair, I flipped it to one side and glanced around the room for better lighting. But Evin's smiling face appeared on the screen, and I forgot about everything else.

"Hi," she said breathlessly, setting up the phone where I could see most of her that wasn't hidden behind the counter. She was wearing a cute matching blue pajama set and was squeezing the excess water from her hair with a towel. "You're finally done for the day?"

Sighing, I nodded. "Yeah, I just got back to my hotel room."

"How was your day? What did you do?"

"I was on a morning show and did some other press interviews. It was a long day, but we had dinner at one of my favorite restaurants in London."

Evin narrowed her eyes and tilted her head. "What time is it there? Like midnight?"

I glanced over at the clock on the bedside table and squinted to make out the time.

"Yeah, a little past."

She dropped her towel on the counter and braced her hands against the sink. "Oh my gosh, Lucy. You should go to sleep."

"I will," I promised with a laugh. "How was your day?"

Evin reached forward and grabbed her purple hairbrush, running it through her brown locks.

"Well, definitely not as interesting as yours. I worked and wrote a little bit. The writer's block has almost completely lifted."

Flipping over onto my back, I held the phone above me as I lay back on the bed. "That's exciting as both your reader and your friend."

She smiled at her phone—at *me*—but quickly looked away as she shook her head.

"It is very exciting after not being able to write for a while, but don't ask for details because there's no way I'm spoiling it." I groaned, and her smile widened. "But you can be one of the first to read it once it's done."

"I bet it's going to be amazing."

"Okay, that's sweet, but if you *are* going to be one of my early readers, you have to give me feedback."

"Then maybe I wouldn't be the best option," I said honestly. Evin dropped her brush on the counter and retrieved her phone from where it was propped against the mirror. "I think everything you write is nothing less than perfect, so…"

Her laugh was a light, sweet sound, and I couldn't remember the last time I'd smiled so much. Talking to Evin was like a breath of fresh air. A reminder of what life could be like.

"I guess if I need a confidence boost, then I know who to talk to," she quipped as she walked through her apartment.

"Yes, I am always good for that. Telling you how amazing and talented you are."

She set the phone back down in the kitchen, facing out toward her living room and the windows lining the exposed brick wall behind her TV. Of the little I'd seen of her apartment, I loved how personal it was. The little touches she'd added and the color everywhere.

She walked out of frame for a moment, giving me an uninhibited shot of her butcher block island, before she returned with a to-go container. Struggling to open it, she squinted her eyes as she peeled the lid back, and I couldn't help but laugh at her expression.

"So, you're in for the night then? No big plans?" I asked. She again stepped out of frame as I heard what sounded like her microwave door open.

"No plans," she hollered. "I have an early breakfast with my family tomorrow morning, so I need to catch up on sleep."

"I think it's so cool that you live so close," I said. She'd told me all about her parents, who still lived in her childhood home, and her older sister, Palmer, who was married and also lived near the city.

"How long has it been since you've seen your family?"

Hoisting myself off the bed, I walked around the perimeter and plopped down near the pillows at the top. I positioned my phone against the lamp and curled up against the headboard.

Sadly, it took me a second to remember the last time I'd seen my family. They'd come out to California late last year, for my birthday, to be exact. My schedule was so chaotic, I didn't have more than two days off at a time, so they came out the day before, and we'd celebrated together.

"My birthday, last August," I said with a sigh. Almost nine months ago. "But it looks like I'll have a few days off in the next month. I plan on making a trip back home and spending whatever time I can with them."

"What do you usually do when you go home?" Evin asked, retrieving her dinner from the microwave and crossing back in front of the phone screen.

I smiled at the thought of my parents' little house in the middle of nowhere. "They live on a bunch of land, so I usually help out with the chores. My mom and I like to drive to the few surrounding towns and check out the antique stores. Honestly, my favorite thing to do is just sit around and play games. My older brother usually comes by, too, and stays for a little while."

"My family's big on game nights, too," Evin said with a smile, moving the phone once again across the kitchen and to the island, where she propped me against something as she slipped into a barstool. She stirred her dinner and lifted a forkful of pasta to her mouth.

She chewed quickly, holding her hand in front of her mouth as she continued speaking. Exhaustion was creeping in. My eyelids were heavy, and my thoughts were lagging. Lagging so much that rather than listening to her speak, I caught myself just watching her.

The way her hazel eyes shined when she spoke about her family and her often shy demeanor morphed when she was excited. I was mesmerized with the way her lips moved, the way they formed around her fork, and the way her throat bobbed as she swallowed.

Fuck, I thought, blinking quickly and straightening to keep myself from nodding off. I couldn't have a crush on Evin. I just couldn't.

Yet, there I was, infatuated by the pretty, intelligent, sweet brunette.

Evin and I talked for a while, discussing our families and childhoods and catching up on anything else that happened that day. But at some point, I lost my battle with exhaustion.

I woke up not an hour later to all the lights in my room still on and in the same position I'd been in. Only my phone was dark.

"Shit," I muttered, and jumped up, reaching for my phone and unlocking it to find two new texts from Evin.

> Evin Morgan: I knew you were going to fall asleep. 😔
>
> Evin Morgan: Good night, Lucy. I'll talk to you tomorrow!

Quickly, I typed out an apology as I headed toward the bathroom and flipped on the light. While I was brushing my teeth, Evin's response appeared across my screen.

> Evin Morgan: No need to be sorry. I knew you were exhausted. I'm glad we got to talk, though. We should FaceTime more often.

My smile was awkward with my toothbrush and toothpaste in my mouth, but I couldn't help it. When she said things like that, it didn't help my crush at all. It actually made it so much worse. And it made me want to find a way to meet her in person. To see if the connection I thought we may share was real or all in my head.

five

. . .

Evin

STANDING in the back room of the bookstore, I snapped a quick selfie in a mirror leaned up against the wall. It wasn't the most flattering photo I'd ever taken, but Lucy was asking about my outfit for my first official signing at a local Dallas bookstore.

The interest she'd drummed up from her interview and subsequent post had really changed the trajectory of my writing career. My publisher was investing more money in me, and I was making more writing than I was at my day job. Although I still wasn't going to quit because I liked the safety net it provided. It was possible that all the success could be temporary and my next book, which I'd finally made headway on, could flop.

Lucy didn't believe that, though. When she'd asked me for my number, I'd been shocked, but once we started texting, we hadn't stopped.

She didn't have a lot of free time, but when she did, she texted me. There was also the odd FaceTime or phone call, but those were harder to come by with her schedule.

Me: This is what I decided on.

I sent the text to Lucy and attached the picture I'd taken. It wasn't anything special, just a black dress and white sneakers, but I felt cute. She was on her way to another appearance, so I didn't expect her to respond so quickly.

> Lucy: You look perfect, Evin. You're going to kill it!

My cheeks heated, and I couldn't suppress the smile that slipped across my face. It had taken a few days for the awe to wear off. For a while, I still couldn't believe I was texting Lucy Lowe. But the more we talked, and the more I learned about her, the more she just became Lucy.

And I understood why the entire world had a crush on her. Staring down at my phone, it hit me once again that I did, too. Not only was she one of the most gorgeous people on the planet, but she was also down-to-earth and kind and funny and charming.

Only I didn't have a crush on Lucy Lowe, the famous actress that won over every person's heart. I had a crush on Lucy from Oklahoma, who loved her dogs and hated peas.

"I know that look," Aiden said as he walked through the door that opened to the actual store. I flipped my best friend off, but all he did was chuckle, grab my hand, and kiss my offending finger. "Sorry, but that's like the fifth time *today* I've caught you smiling at your phone. If you don't want me to comment on it, don't look so smitten every time you text her."

I shook my head and slid my phone into my convenient dress pocket. "I can't," I began and groaned. "I can't help it."

Aiden wrapped his arms around me and squeezed hard. I wasn't necessarily short, but he was tall, so my face pressed directly against his chest and I tried to prevent my makeup from smudging.

"Our little Evin Morgan is in love," he cooed, and I fought for a second before he finally freed me.

"I'm not in love, Aiden. I have a crush, that's all."

"A crush on Lucy Lowe, don't we all?"

I smoothed my dress down and glanced in the mirror one last time. "You have a crush on her, too?"

Aiden chuckled and plopped down in a chair in the corner. "Not like that," he said, folding his arms in his lap. "But Lucy is beautiful. Anyone who tells you they think otherwise is lying. Just because I'm into guys doesn't mean I can't appreciate a beautiful woman."

His smile was easy, and I understood what he meant. Aiden was the only person who knew I was texting Lucy. He was a vault, so I knew the information was safe with him. We'd been best friends since childhood, and I knew he wouldn't tell anyone for clout or to seem cool.

He was also one of the only people I'd come out to. It wasn't until a year ago just after my twenty-seventh birthday that I was honest with myself about my sexuality. Up until then I'd only been in relationships or slept with men, but something changed. I wasn't sure what the catalyst was, but one day I realized that all those feelings I'd had for men, I could also have for a woman.

I knew my parents would be supportive, but I just hadn't found the right time to tell them. Aiden, on the other hand, learned about it over our second bottle of sake at one of our favorite restaurants when we were having dinner with my sister, Palmer.

Palmer was ecstatic, but Aiden had whooped and gotten the attention of the entire restaurant. He understood better than most. He also hadn't come out until his twenties and helped me through the identity crisis that followed.

"You know she likes women, right?" he asked with a smile. I gave him an unimpressed look and shook my head. Of course I knew that. Everyone knew that, and I'd thought about it a lot more than I wanted to admit.

"Anyway, Marianne said she'll be back here in five minutes

to get you. The line is down the street and around the block," he said.

I whipped around and braced my hand on my stomach, which was trying to heave itself out of my body. "No, it's not."

Aiden nodded slowly and smiled like a proud dad. "This is going to be epic, Evin. They're worried they don't have enough books."

"Oh my god, I'm going to puke," I mumbled. On the other side of the door, I could hear commotion and Marianne's voice welcoming people into the store. She gave them instructions on where to stand and explained that I'd have a few minutes to spend with each reader. "How—how did I get here? I'm not—this isn't going to work. They're going to be so disappointed in me. What if I'm not what they expected?"

Aiden stood and braced his palms against each of my cheeks, forcing me to crane my neck to look up at him. He led me through several deep breaths, and once I'd stopped hyperventilating, he dropped his hands to clasp mine.

"You are going to be great, Evin. You are the best, and all those people out there are about to experience it. Now, we're going to leave the impostor syndrome in here when we go greet your adoring fans."

I groaned one more time for good measure and did a nervous little jig to get out the rest of the anxious energy. Aiden rolled his lips to keep from laughing but nodded.

Behind me there was a knock on the door, and I turned in time to see Marianne, the owner of the bookstore, peeking her head inside. "We're ready whenever you are, Ms. Morgan."

"Thanks, I'll just be another minute."

She smiled and shut the door behind her. I reached back into my pocket and pulled my phone out one more time and planned to read the text from Lucy again only to find she'd sent another one.

Lucy: I know you're probably freaking out, and I understand that feeling better than most. But I promise, you were meant to do this. You're an amazing writer and person. Each one of those readers is lucky to meet the great Evin Morgan!

six
. . .

Evin

"I LOVE BEING RIGHT," Aiden said as I dropped into the chair I'd barely sat in all night. It was behind the table they'd set up for me, but I couldn't properly greet people from the opposite side.

I'd hugged so many people and signed so many books that my hand was permanently cramping and my cheeks hurt from smiling. But it had gone better than I ever could have imagined. I couldn't stop freaking smiling. Even when Aiden was gloating.

Marianne stopped on the other side of the table and clapped her hands together. "We actually have one more reader that would like to meet you."

I was so tired, but still, I perked up. Glancing around her, I looked toward the front of the store. "Okay, no problem. Umm… are they here?"

On cue, the back door opened and a very large man wearing all black stepped into the store. I stood and peeked around the bookshelf that was partially blocking my view. My feet ached, but I pushed the pain to the back of my mind.

He wasn't my average reader, and I very quickly realized he didn't care anything about seeing me as his gaze swept across the store, like he was noting the exits and each person inside. He nodded once and spoke into an earpiece before he stepped aside.

I quickly looked at Aiden, but all he did was shrug. He came to stand beside me, and I looked up just in time to see Lucy walk through the back door.

My heart immediately started pounding, and suddenly, I was lightheaded. Everything else in the bookstore faded—Aiden next to me, the security that filed in around the perimeter of the store, the few employees still left—they'd all vanished. All there was was Lucy walking toward me, a smile slowly spreading across her face.

Fuck, she was even prettier in person. Pretty wasn't even descriptive enough to describe her beauty, but it was all I could think in that moment with my brain working double-time just to put that little thought together.

Her long, black hair was curled and pinned out of her face. She was wearing thick black boots, a dark pink leather skirt, and a black lace top. Her lips matched the color of the skirt, and her eye makeup was smoky, showing off the otherworldly green of her eyes.

She stopped in front of me, and I knew I had to get my shit together. Which was going to prove exceptionally difficult when all I could think was: *holy fucking shit.* Over and over again.

"Hi, Evin. I'm sorry I'm late."

Holy fucking shit. Holy fucking shit.

Her voice was sultry and a little husky. Like it was a soft blanket warmed by a fire that beckoned you to snuggle beneath it. Clearing my throat, I straightened and chastised myself for being so ridiculous. I could handle this. I would handle it.

"Well, you were kind of busy," I said, and I was impressed with how level my voice sounded. It wasn't nearly as confident as Lucy's, but I never expected that much.

She smiled, flashing her straight, white teeth, and laughed. The sound was just as rich as her voice, and I felt it through my entire body.

"I heard you sold out," she said.

"I guess we did. If I'd known you were coming—"

"Oh, no," Marianne chimed in. "We put some aside for Ms. Lowe and her group."

Lucy turned that charming smile on Marianne, and even the older owner blushed under her gaze. "Thank you so much for doing that. You received the payment and everything, right?"

Marianne nodded emphatically and hurried off to retrieve the books Lucy had purchased at some point.

Beside me, Aiden cleared his throat. I'd honestly forgotten he was standing there and jumped at the sound.

"Oh, shit. Lucy, this is my best friend, Aiden."

Aiden stuck out his hand, and Lucy shook it. "I've heard so much about you. It's nice to finally meet you," she said.

I didn't miss his knowing side-eye, and I tried not to blush. Aiden was one of the most important people in my life. Of course, I told Lucy about him.

"It's great to meet you, too. I've also heard *so* much about you."

Then it was Lucy's turn to glance over at me, and fucking hell, I couldn't help the blush that heated my cheeks. I just hoped my makeup covered up the worst of it.

"Excuse us," one of the employees said to my right. I glanced their way and saw a huge stack of books in his arms. "Can I just —" He nodded to the table.

"Yes, yes," I said quickly, moving out of the way.

He set his stack of books down, and three more people followed him with similar stacks. They each smiled and waved to Lucy, and she graciously smiled and waved back.

I looked from her to the books and back again.

"These are all for you?"

Lucy shrugged and reached for one of the books, picking it up and flipping through the pages as she held it to her nose. Old books, new books, whichever they may be, I loved the smell, too.

"They're for my entire team, my family, any friends. I just wanted to...support you."

A nervous giggle erupted from my lips, and I sat back down in the chair behind the table. Lucy took the other one Aiden had been sitting in all evening, and I chastised myself for my awkwardness. *It was just Lucy*, I reminded myself. She was my...friend. My very famous, very hot friend, but my *friend*, nonetheless.

"Well, I hope they enjoy them. Or have read them before. This is a lot of books," I said. I picked up the first one and poised my pen over the title page. "Wait, you do want all of them signed, right?"

She laughed and slid the book she'd been holding back on the table. "Yes, of course."

I signed two and started a new, neat stack on the other side of the table. Because I couldn't keep my eyes to myself, I looked back up at her. Lucy seemed to be having the same problem. She was just watching me with a little smile tilting her lips. I cleared my throat and grabbed a third book.

"I didn't think you were in Texas. Weren't you just in Oklahoma visiting your family?"

Out of the corner of my eye, I saw her nod. "I was, but I left a little early to come see you. They understood when I explained why I had to come."

My pen froze midair, and I peeked up at her without moving my head. I signed the book and set it aside before grabbing another.

"So, you told your family about me?"

"Of course," she said like it wasn't a big deal. She crossed one leg over the other and sat back in her chair. The movement was casual, but all I could think about was how it put her so much closer to me and showed off the long lines of her legs.

"My mom asked me if your books were as good as I made them out to be, and I made her immediately download the ebooks. I'll send her a few of the signed ones as well. I told her they were better than I probably described and that the author was just as incredible."

Suddenly very hot, I tossed my hair over my shoulders and ignored the way my body reacted to her compliments.

"So, tonight went well?" she asked, and I appreciated the topic change.

"It really did. I didn't expect so many people to show up. I mean, I know my sales have gone up since you posted, but it was something else to see it in person and talk to people who have read or want to read what I've written."

"What was your favorite part of the night? Did anything stick out?"

Still making my way through the never-ending pile of books in front of me, I contemplated her questions only for a moment. "This woman, Sandy, said she hadn't picked up a book in over two decades because she used to read with her husband before he passed away. But her granddaughter sent her one of mine, and she thought she'd give it a try. She said my book got her back into reading and that her husband would have loved them just as much."

"Oh, wow," Lucy muttered. "That's so beautiful."

"I know. I cried," I said with a laugh. "So, where are you off to next? Do you get any other significant time off?"

She tapped her booted foot and shook her head. "Nope, not for a few weeks, but tomorrow I'm going to New York to do the *Super Late Show*."

I laughed as I set the final book on the pile and recapped my pen. "I love that show. He's freaking hilarious."

"It is one of my preferred shows. The late shows usually keep things light and fluffy, which is a nice change of pace."

"I'm sure. I saw the one a few days ago where they asked some...really gross questions."

She shrugged and tried to appear unaffected—just as she had during the interview—but I could tell it bothered her. He'd asked about her having to cut weight for the role, and implied that maybe it was a good thing she'd lost a few pounds.

"Yeah, well, that's part of the gig, I guess. Thankfully, those interviews are becoming less and less common." I sat the last book on the pile to my left and recapped my pen only to be stopped by Lucy with her hand on my forearm. "I actually have one more book for you to sign," she said. Like they'd coordinated it, a woman with platinum-blonde hair pulled back in a bun strode toward us and handed Lucy another book.

"Hi, I'm Madison," the woman said, reaching her hand forward. I shook it, and she offered a tight-lipped smile. "Lucy's manager."

"It's so nice to meet you. I'm—"

"Oh, trust me," she said quickly. "I know who you are." It didn't seem rude, just like she was stating a fact. She glanced over at Lucy once before she headed back toward one of the security people near the back of the store.

"Madison wasn't super excited when I told her we'd started texting," she explained. "Not because she doesn't like *you*, she just was worried, I guess. My having friends isn't as important to her as, well, my safety."

Friend. That's what we were, I reminded myself. Friends.

"Anyway," she continued, glancing down at the book in her hands, it was one of the few glimpses of vulnerability I'd seen from her. "This is the copy of your first book I bought from that little indie bookstore. It's very well loved, but I was hoping you could sign it. And write whatever else you want to."

She handed it to me, and she was right—it looked very well loved. The pages were worn, and the cover was creased. There was a little water and sun damage, but it was proof of how much she'd loved it. How many times she'd read it.

Emotion sat thick at the back of my throat, and I felt the pressure to come up with something incredible to write on the spot. It had to be epic and eloquent. It had to live up to any and all expectations she had.

I was silently spiraling, staring down at the empty title page and tapping my pen against the table, when Lucy's hand appeared. She curved her fingers over mine and halted my pen tapping.

"You can think about it," she offered.

"I would like to, but you said you're leaving tomorrow, so I need to—"

"Have dinner with me."

My eyes bounced to hers, and she chuckled, probably at my shocked expression. She didn't remove her hand from around mine.

"Sorry, what I meant to say was, would you like to come have dinner with me? I have the night free, and I already made reservations at that restaurant you told me about. The one that you and Aiden love."

"Wait, really? You want me to have dinner with you?"

She nodded. "Yes. I have the rest of the night to myself, but I'd much rather spend it with you."

I sucked in a sharp breath and lost myself in her sincere, depthless green eyes. Her fingers were warm against mine, and for a moment, I let myself consider what they might feel like elsewhere. Her long, pretty fingers in my hair or wrapping around my hips.

It was such a good thought, I fought the shiver that wanted to rack my body.

Instead, I smiled. "Has anyone ever said 'no' to Lucy Lowe?"

seven

. . .

Lucy

USHERED BY MY SECURITY, we both slid into the back seat of the SUV and were pulling out of the alley behind the bookstore in a few seconds.

"I feel like I need to warn you," I said as we turned onto the main street. "We're going to go in a back entrance and into a private room set up for us. But there's still a possibility there will be paparazzi and other people taking photos. I've kind of gotten used to it now, but if you don't want that, we can do something else. Anything else."

Evin clicked her seat belt for the short drive and turned her kind, hazel eyes on me. "I'm sure it'll be fine."

"You say that, but—"

She stopped me with her hand on top of mine—just like I'd done earlier. "I promise, I'll be okay. You live with it all the time, I can live with it for one night."

God, she was so sweet. Too sweet.

She'd been stressed about what to wear to her signing, but Evin was so beautiful it wouldn't have mattered what she wore. I could imagine her in an old movie, the black and white not doing her any justice. Her chocolate-brown hair looked just as soft in person—the waves brushing the tops of her breasts—and her cheeks blushed so prettily.

Over our few FaceTime calls and the photos we'd sent back and forth, I'd wondered about a little scar above her lip. If it was the work of shadow, but it was really there in the center of her Cupid's bow.

It was cute and even more prominent when her plump lips curved into a smile. I wanted to taste her smile. I bet it would be just as sweet.

"You may change your mind, and if you do, that's okay."

She shook her head and looked down at where our hands were touching. I didn't want her to stop touching me, but I knew a second before it happened that she'd pull away. When she did, I ignored the small ache in my chest. All I wanted her to do was keep touching me.

Although I didn't know if she'd be totally interested in that.

It was well-known that I was exclusively attracted to women, a fact I learned very early in life. But in all the time we'd talked, Evin hadn't mentioned her sexuality. And I wasn't one to push, so I'd patiently wait for her to share when or if she was ready. I had a feeling, though, and I was right most of the time. Except for when I was wrong.

And I really hoped I wasn't wrong, because my crush had grown into so much more.

I truly liked Evin, and I refused to do anything to fuck it up. Even if we did just end up friends, I wanted her in my life. Her kindness and sweetness were fucking contagious.

"No, I—I—" she began and shook her head. "Never mind."

"Finish your sentence. What were you going to say?" Not always, but occasionally, Evin was shy, and when she glanced back up at me, I could see how self-conscious she was. But she took a breath and fidgeted with the hem of her dress in her lap.

"I'm not going to change my mind, was all I was going to say.

You're here, and I want—I want to spend time with you, too. Especially since this is your one free night."

A feeling I hadn't experienced in a while—that hopeful, giddy feeling you get when something is just starting—spread through my chest.

"Perfect."

Getting into the restaurant wasn't a big deal. No one knew we were coming, and the staff did a fantastic job ushering us to our private room. Except the room wasn't as private as I thought, and there were only curtains separating us from the rest of the dining room. Partially sheer curtains that wanted to fly open every time someone walked past.

We both slid into the circular booth, ending up in the center directly next to one another. It would have been intimate if there weren't people trying to sneak a peek inside. I was used to the attention, but I didn't want to scare Evin off. It was a lot to get used to.

"I've never been back here before," Evin said. "We usually sit at the bar. One of our friends from high school used to work here and gave us free drinks all the time."

Our waiter pushed through the curtains and handed us two menus and set a third—the drink menu—down in the center.

"We're so excited you decided to dine with us this evening, Ms. Lowe. Can I get you anything to drink to start?"

Immediately, I peered over at Evin. "What's your favorite?"

She pursed her lips and narrowed her eyes as she grabbed the drink menu. "I like this one," she said, pointing to the third one on the list. "The Nigori."

"We'll take that then. The bottle, please."

"Great choice," he agreed and promised to be back shortly.

"Okay, now, you have to order all your favorites," I prompted. "I want to try everything."

Evin laughed and opened the very large menu. All I could think, though, was how much I wanted to hear her laugh over and over again. It was light and airy. Like pure joy was lingering in each note.

She tucked her hair behind her ear and began describing each of her favorite dishes. I listened, of course, and noted each dish she mentioned, but I also couldn't stop staring at her profile. The cute little bump in her nose and the way it ever so slightly tilted up at the end. I loved watching her lower, plumper lip press against the top one as she spoke and her long, dark lashes flutter together.

"But that would be a lot of food," she said and turned to me, catching me staring.

I played it off with a smile, and I liked the way her eyes dropped to my lips as they tilted.

"We can get everything. I'm starving."

She began to argue, but our waiter interrupted with the bottle we ordered and two glasses.

"Did we decide on any appetizers?"

"Actually, I think we're ready to order," I said and recited each dish Evin had mentioned. The waiter nodded, retrieved our menus, and retreated back out the curtain. I locked eyes with a younger woman who was so excited to see me, she bounced in her seat and leaned forward to tell the rest of her table.

The curtain fell back into place before I could wave. And I forgot just as quickly about everything on the other side. Especially when the most intriguing person I'd ever met was seated right next to me.

"You just ordered so much food," Evin muttered. "We're never going to eat all that."

I shrugged and picked up my glass. "I want to try your favorite food, and I want to do it right." I held up my glass, and Evin caught on, quickly picking hers up.

"What are we toasting to?" she asked with a smile.

A million different suggestions ran through my mind, none of which were very appropriate. Apparently, I lingered too long on the thought, and Evin jumped in for me.

"What about, to…" she began. "Kismet."

Her expression was tentative, but when I smiled, that apprehension disappeared. Kismet—I remembered the first time I'd said it in one of our earliest messages. It seemed to fit so well.

"To kismet," I repeated, and we tapped our glasses together. I took a sip, and the fruity, sweet flavor hit my tongue. I groaned at how good it was and then took a second, longer sip. "Oh my gosh, this is amazing."

I looked up to find Evin staring at me, lower lip trapped between her teeth and pupils wide. My pulse raced, and I stopped breathing altogether. I was still holding the glass midair, and I refused to move. I wanted her to keep looking at me like that—like she was contemplating what my lips would feel like against hers—and I worried if I moved, the spell might break.

But she eventually cleared her throat and slipped her glass back onto the table.

"I really can't believe you're here," she said. "And that you're *real*."

I laughed and dabbed my napkin over my mouth. "We've had video calls and phone calls, you knew I was real."

She shrugged and ran her finger around the perimeter of her glass. "Yes, but artificial intelligence is really good nowadays. I guess I wasn't going to *truly* believe it until I could reach out and touch you."

Yes, touch me. Please touch me, I thought but refrained from saying out loud.

"Well, people have tried to use my likeness for AI and many other things, but as you now know, I am very real."

eight

. . .

Evin

"YOUR PARENTS HAVE BEEN TRAVELING A LOT?" Lucy asked as she popped another piece of sushi in her mouth.

Dinner was going so well. She was just as kind and generous as she was over the phone, which was a pleasant surprise.

"Yeah, I still try to see them at least once a month, same with my sister, but now that we're both out of the house, they're using their free time to travel to all the places they've ever wanted to go and enjoying being empty nesters."

Lucy nodded and finished chewing. "My parents did the same thing when I left at eighteen. But when my brother left, they converted his bedroom into my dad's den like two weeks later. He still hasn't let them live that down."

"I think that's so cool that you're still so close to your family," I said, and I could tell immediately my words hit some sort of a nerve. She dropped her head and used her chopsticks to push a piece of rice around her plate. Immediately, I tried to backtrack. "Shit, I didn't mean—"

She looked up and furrowed her dark brows, waving off what was about to be a stuttered apology.

"Oh, no. It's fine, and you're right—I'm still really close to them, which makes it even harder to be away."

I set my utensils down and leaned back in the booth. At some point, we'd both turned so we were facing one another. The circular booth would have made it a little awkward if it were anyone else. But Lucy was…well, she was her, and I liked being close.

"Have you thought about moving back, or do you have to be in LA?"

She also dropped her chopsticks and mimicked my position. Her right leg was bent on top of the cushion, and she let the side of her head rest against the back of the booth.

"I think about it all the time. I love what I do but don't love where I live. LA started out as a convenient thing, but even so, I couldn't move back too close to them. They live over an hour away from any major airports, and I need to be more accessible than that. Otherwise, I'm going to spend more time traveling than I'd like."

"So, maybe not in Oklahoma, but somewhere else could be an option," I offered. I couldn't imagine being too far away from my family. They were the best support system, and I also really loved Dallas, so it worked out well.

She nodded. "Yeah, that could work. Although my team would freak. I don't know," she said, glancing around and then down at her hands. "I kind of like Dallas."

Even if I wanted to, I couldn't hide my excitement at her just mentioning the smallest possibility of moving to my city. My imagination ran wild with the idea.

"I'd have to show you more of the city, though, before you decided."

"Of course, I'd want to make an informed decision," she volleyed back with a smile. "Where would you take me?"

I didn't even think, I just started listing some of my favorite places and areas, ticking off each one with my fingers and doing my best to sell it before she even saw it.

"And I love the little town where my parents live," I said at the end. "We'd have to make a stop there."

I didn't say anything else. I let my statement linger in the air around us and thoughtfully gauged her reaction. Her eyes widened, although subtly, and her lips curved.

"You'd take me to meet your parents?"

"Of course." My response was automatic and genuine. Lucy glanced up at me and opened her mouth like she was about to say something, only for our waiter to slip through the curtain at that exact moment.

"Sorry to interrupt," he said, stopping short and glancing between us. It was then that I realized our posture was very intimate—how we faced one another and how close we were. I didn't want to move, but I did straighten as he took another step. "Can I get you anything else?"

I scanned the array of mostly empty plates as Lucy asked, "Do you want anything else, Evin?"

I shook my head. "Nope, I don't think I could eat anything else even if I wanted to."

"My assistant will take care of the check," Lucy said, and the waiter nodded and left before I realized what happened.

"Wait, we should split it, right?" I asked because it was the polite thing to do. However, I wasn't totally sure if I could cover half without being in a pinch until payday.

"Umm...no, we're not going to split it. This was my idea, and I invited you, which means I pay." There was no room for argument in her voice, and I honestly didn't want to argue anyway.

And I really didn't want the night to end. "Well, thank you so much. I've really had the best time."

"Evin," Lucy began, and I liked the way my name sounded on her lips. Especially in her sultry, husky voice. "I honestly don't want to say goodbye yet. This is the most fun I've had in... well, in forever."

"I also don't want to say goodbye," I admitted. "And usually,

I would recommend that we go to a bar, but I don't think that's a good idea."

With Lucy in front of me, it was easy to give her my undivided attention. She was beautiful and enigmatic, but every once in a while, I still felt the eyes of the other diners behind that sheer curtain. And behind her, through a window looking out onto a side street, people had already begun lining up. Thankfully they couldn't see in, but I could absolutely see them.

Lucy followed my gaze and glanced behind her. She shook her head and cringed when she saw the chaos beyond the window.

"Unfortunately, that's not an option for me, and I forgot my disguise at my hotel room."

"Do you actually go out in disguise?"

She laughed and brushed her hair out of her face. "Yes, I have. I usually bring some sort of wig with me everywhere I go. I was actually thinking maybe we could go back to my hotel. I have booze, and we're guaranteed not to be interrupted there."

It was a little scary how much I wanted to go with her. It was scary how much I wanted to be *actually* alone with no prying eyes or possibility of interruption.

Trying to play it cool, I fixed a smile to my face and said again, "Has anyone ever said 'no' to Lucy Lowe?"

nine

. . .

Lucy

"I'M NOT COMPLAINING or trying to be rude," Evin said as we stepped off the elevator and across the hallway to my suite. "But I don't know how you handle that every day. It's like you can't go anywhere without people recognizing you and swarming."

I sighed and unlaced my boots right inside the door, kicking them off toward the bedroom and wiggling my aching toes.

"It's a lot, but I know that most of them have good intentions. It also gets worse when I have a new project. They just want a picture or an autograph. I've more or less gotten used to it, but it's not for everyone. I've figured that out the hard way."

The last sentence sounded so much sadder than I meant it to. Yeah, it was hard, but I didn't want to ruin the night by playing the *"poor me, I'm rich and famous and can't go grocery shopping"* game.

"I don't know," Evin said as she followed me into the little kitchen, her black dress swirling around her. "I would think that if that person really wanted to, they could get on board. It's a change, but that's kind of what life's about: things are constantly changing, and you just have to take it as it comes."

I grabbed two tiny bottles of liquor from the mini bar—bypassing the larger bottles on the counter—and turned to find her leaning against the counter, elbows on the granite and her eyes on me.

"That was very insightful, Ms. Morgan," I joked. "Very wise."

She rolled her eyes and took the little bottle I offered her. "I'm always very insightful and wise, Ms. Lowe. You'll learn that about me."

We tapped our bottles together and threw them back. The tequila burned on the way down and settled warmly in my stomach. Her reaction to her own shot was freaking adorable. The way her nose scrunched and her eyes screwed closed.

"I feel like I already know you pretty well," I said, taking her empty bottle and tossing it in the trash. "We've been talking for two months. That's a pretty good amount of time."

Evin pursed her lips and turned to take in the rest of the suite. It was the penthouse, which was less a luxury than a necessity since you needed a badge to get up here.

The suite was very nice with luxurious cream couches and matching curtains. It was a little plain for my taste, but it was still pretty.

"Two months is a good amount of time," she said, walking beside the couch and running her hand along the back.

"I know that you're ready to quit your day job and pursue writing full-time, but you're nervous about putting all your eggs in one basket, so to say." She stopped on the other side of the couch and put her hands in the pockets of her dress.

"Your favorite song is 'Iris' by the Goo Goo Dolls, and you eat ketchup on your eggs, which I still find absolutely appalling."

She quirked a smile, and her tinkling laughter filtered through the room. I grabbed two waters from the fridge and crossed to her. I rounded the couch and plopped down on one side, setting her water on the coffee table in front of us.

"You'd certainly win an Evin trivia game," she said as she sat down on the opposite side. She was too far away, but moving now would make it too obvious, so I waited.

"And I know that your favorite song is 'Smells Like Teen Spirit' by Nirvana, and you prefer crunchy peanut butter."

I tossed my head back and laughed toward the ceiling, curling my legs underneath me and resting my arm on the back of the couch. "And that's all we'll ever need to know," I joked.

She took a swig of her water and recapped it. Messing with the label, I could feel her thinking.

"So, maybe tell me something you haven't told anyone else? Something I don't know and most people wouldn't?"

I twirled a piece of hair around my fingers and stared out the windows behind her that looked out onto the Dallas skyline. It was that time of night where the lights were slowly winking out, and I imagined all the people in their own homes and the different, exciting lives they lived.

Digging deep, the first thing I thought of was definitely something I'd never voiced, and honestly never thought I'd tell anyone. When I looked back at Evin and her sweet, open expression, I wanted to tell her. I trusted her with my secrets.

"I'm worried I'll never know real love," I admitted. "I'm worried that I—my lifestyle and job—will be too much for some people, and others will only want me for the things I can provide. It feels impossible to know if anyone is ever genuine."

In a move I wasn't expecting, Evin scooted closer and took my hand in both of hers. I held my breath as I looked up at her and tried like hell to control my wild pulse.

"That sounds miserable," she said quietly.

All I could do was nod and look back down at our hands. Her hazel eyes were piercing, like she was seeing too much of me, parts I'd never allowed another person to witness. And I was enthralled with the way she felt. Even if it was just her hands, I was already obsessed. They were soft and tentative but steady.

"I think you'll know," she continued. "I know that sounds

really unhelpful, and it's okay to protect your heart, but I like to think that when it happens, when it's genuine, you'll know."

It was a sweet sentiment, and I hoped she was right. Although I'd been duped several times before. But I didn't feel like going through my dating history when the only woman I wanted to think about was sitting in front of me, holding my hand, and looking better than anyone ever had a right to look.

"I hope so," I said with a deep breath. "Now, your turn."

I squeezed her hand, and she matched my deep breath with one of her own. She closed her eyes as she said, "I'm bi...sexual. Bisexual."

Rolling my lips, I tried to contain my smile. Fuck, she was so cute.

When I didn't say anything, she peeked one eye open, then the other. "Why are you smiling?"

"I'm not smiling," I said through what was absolutely the beginning of a smile.

"Oh my gosh, you're trying so hard not to smile. What's so funny about that?" She tossed one hand into the air in exasperation but left the other clasped in mine.

"No, I'm not smiling because it's funny. I'm smiling because...I kind of already knew."

"I swear," she sighed. She dropped her head back against the couch and groaned to the ceiling. "You pour your heart out to me, and I tell you something you already know. I mean, not even my parents know. You're the third person I've told."

I placed a hand over my heart. "I'm honored. Was Aiden the first?"

She nodded without picking up her head. "Yeah, I only told him and my sister a year ago. I didn't really figure it out until just after my birthday. My sister was accepting and excited, but Aiden was *crazy* excited. Jumping for joy and whooping."

I laughed because I could picture it, but I also had a hard time thinking about that large man jumping for joy. "Well, I'm honored to be the third person, and welcome to our little club."

She rolled her head to the side and narrowed her eyes. "How did you know?" she asked.

She sat up, and I battled with what to tell her. The truth would put us in new territory. Right now, we were tiptoeing around flirting—using double meaning to our advantage and testing the physical waters by holding hands and sitting close. Long looks and soft smiles were enough.

The truth would take us from tiptoeing to an all-out sprint.

"I just have a sense for these things. You know, being into women myself."

Evin nodded, but her eyes told me something else entirely. "Sure, but why don't I believe you?"

Probably because that was only half the truth, I thought. Sighing, I turned her hand over in my lap and ran my finger over the defined lines on her palm, then up and down each finger. I heard her sharp intake of breath, but I didn't look up.

"You really want to know," I asked, and her "yes" was automatic, although soft. She readjusted, pulling her leg closer over the other, and I wondered if she was trying to relieve growing pressure between her thighs.

Looking back up, our eyes locked, and I hoped like hell I was right. Her eyes were intent on my face, and her breathing was labored.

"Because you look at me how I imagine I look at you."

She hummed in the back of her throat. "And how exactly am I looking at you?" Her voice was soft and breathy. And her eyes watched my mouth as I licked my lips.

"Like you're dying to know what my lips feel like or how they taste. Like you're considering how it would feel to touch me or be touched by me."

Her breath caught, and her lips parted. I considered her expression and only found desire stirring behind her heavy-lidded eyes. Reaching forward, I tucked a piece of hair behind her ear and ran my fingers down the soft strands where they ended just above her breast.

"Unless you tell me 'no' in the next two seconds, I'm going to kiss you, Evin."

My hand shifted, and I cradled her cheek. It took more than two seconds for me to lean forward because I did so slowly, carefully. I wanted to give her time to pull away if she wanted to. But she didn't.

Our lips brushed softly together, and my entire body sighed in relief. She felt better than my wildest imagination could have conjured. She was cautious, but that was fine—I would be confident enough for both of us. Because I'd never wanted someone so bad.

I shifted closer, and she tightened her hold on my other hand still sitting in my lap.

Worried that I'd pushed it too far, I pulled back just enough to see her face. Her eyes fluttered open, and she ran her tongue across her lips.

"What are you doing? Why'd you stop?"

"I just wanted to make sure you're good."

She cracked a small smile and lifted her hand to my own cheek. "I'm so good, Lucy," she said as she leaned forward and kissed me. *Hard.*

ten

. . .

Evin

I CUPPED her cheeks and slanted my mouth over hers. Once I got over the shock that she was kissing me, I didn't hold back.

She tilted her head and swiped her tongue across my lower lip. I moaned as I opened for her. One hand tangled in the back of my hair as the other slipped down my side and gripped my hip.

"I've been thinking about this all night," she said. "Actually, I've been thinking about this since the first time we FaceTimed."

"Me, too," I agreed automatically.

She felt so good, and she smelled freaking amazing. Like something warm and spicy, and I wanted to breathe her in all the damn time. She tugged me closer, and I pressed up onto my knees.

"Come here," she demanded, guiding me to straddle her hips. Our kiss didn't stop, and there was no hesitation on my part either. I'd never done more than kiss a woman, but with Lucy, everything felt so right, I couldn't second guess it.

My dress flared out around me as I settled on top of her. My hands slipped into her hair, and I raked my fingers through the thick, soft strands. I'd been fantasizing about touching it all night. More accurately, I'd been fantasizing about *her* all night.

Her hands roamed down my body, over the side of each breast and the smallest part of my waist before they finally settled on my hips. Her fingers splayed out and brushed the top of my ass, and I wished my dress wasn't so bulky. I wanted her hands on my bare skin, and when she dug her nails into the fabric, I wanted to feel them biting into me.

Needy, desperate moans left us both as our tongues tangled, and I was growing wetter by the second. My desire had begun as an ember the moment I saw her in the bookstore, but with every word and touch and kiss, it flared brighter and hotter. Now, it was a blue flame burning wild and unencumbered.

She nipped at my lower lip, and my hips bucked in response.

"You're gorgeous, Evin," Lucy muttered against my mouth.

I smiled and rocked my hips again, eager for release. All hesitation, all anxiety about what I was doing for the first time, had burned up with that blazing desire.

Lucy made me feel comfortable and wanted. That made it even easier to let go.

"I'm a writer. I studied literature and languages, yet I can't think of a single word in any language that describes how perfect you are."

Her wide, green eyes bounced between mine, and her hold on me tightened as she licked her kiss-swollen lips. "Keep talking like that, and I'm not going to be able to take this slow much longer."

"I don't want to go slow," I said, letting my hands slide down the sides of her neck and rest against her chest. I could barely make out her heartbeat against my palm, but it felt like it was almost as fast as mine.

She kissed me softly and dropped her hands to the exposed skin of my thighs just below the hem of my dress. "You keep grinding against me like you want something."

I nodded and sucked in a sharp breath as her hands inched

higher up my skirt. Soft hands against my bare skin, I shivered at the sensation.

"Are you wound up? Do you need release?"

I couldn't find words, so I nodded again. She tapped the outside of my thigh and instructed me to put one of my legs between hers.

"Now, press your pussy against my thigh and ride it until you come for me. You think you can get off like that?"

I was so turned on, so primed for pleasure, I swore I could get off if she'd just breathed on me a certain way. But instead of saying that, I nodded again.

"Good. Now, do it," she said as she resumed her ascent up my skirt.

I braced one hand against the side of her neck and the other on her shoulder as I tentatively ground myself against her thigh. The cotton lace of my panties rubbed against me, and I could feel her tights beneath me, too. But she was warm, and just the idea that I was so turned on I was willing to rub myself against her to get off was so fucking hot.

I felt like a slut, and I probably looked like one, too. But Lucy looked like she enjoyed the view. Her lips were parted, and her eyes raked up and down my body as my movements became more confident.

The slip of lace against my clit was torturous, and the pressure of her thigh was just enough to get me there.

"I need to see your pretty pink panties," she murmured, her hands wrapping around the highest part of my thighs where my legs met my hips. She fit her hands in the curve of my body and splayed her fingers around toward my ass.

A light, amused chuckle sprang from my lips, and my voice was breathy when I asked, "How do you know they're pink?"

She smiled and leaned up to kiss me. "I saw them at the restaurant. You shifted, and your dress had ridden up just enough to flash me a little peek of the pink lace between your legs."

I would have been mortified, but I couldn't be when I was shamelessly humping her leg.

"You should take more than a peek."

She nodded and held my stare as she pushed my dress up until the fabric was gathered in her hands and over my hips. Until she could see the thin pink lace covering my pussy.

She dropped her gaze, and I slowed my movements—although it ached to do so. I wanted to give her the best view, so I leaned back and held onto the arm of the couch.

My skin heated under her stare, and I swore I could feel it between my legs. Desire burned bright behind her eyes, and I was so close. Like a rubber band that was poised to snap at any moment, pulled to its limit.

As if she were transfixed by the way my pink, lace-covered pussy ground against her darker tights, she managed to keep my dress pushed back while she ran her thumbs against the edges of my panties and achingly close to where I wanted her the most.

She caressed me and raked her eyes up and down my body like she'd never seen something so gorgeous.

"So sweet. So gorgeous," she muttered as the thought crossed my mind.

Her praise made my cunt clench, and I was so needy, I moved faster against her.

"Grinding on my thigh like a pretty little slut. You look so good, Evin. I can't wait to taste you and touch you everywhere. I want to spend the entire night kissing every inch of your body," she murmured.

She leaned forward and placed one kiss on the top of my breast. That was all it took for me to explode.

eleven

. . .

Lucy

EVIN THREW HER HEAD BACK, hands grappling for something to hold on to, she gripped the side of my neck and the arm of the couch. Her body tensed, and her thighs tightened as the prettiest, most delectable sounds leaped from her lips.

I was so obsessed with her. Everything about her pulled me in. She was so kind, and she looked so sweet, but she hopped on my lap like she'd been thinking about it all night, too.

Her head dropped back down, and her chest heaved as her eyes slowly slid open, and a smile slipped across her lips.

"Holy fucking shit." Her voice was breathy, and her cheeks were flushed. "I've never come so hard before."

I could feel my devious smile growing. "That's nothing, sweet girl. When I get my face between your legs, you're going to come twice as hard."

"You sound so confident," she said, running her hand down the side of my face and tentatively against my chest.

I moaned and wished she'd keep going. "I am."

"I want..." she began, but her words trailed off as her eyes followed the direction of her hand toward my cleavage. She swallowed and took a deep breath. When her eyes flashed to mine, she continued. "It's your turn."

"My turn?"

She nodded and slipped off my thigh, standing on shaky legs and offering me her hand as her dress fell back around her hips. There wasn't a possibility, in any world, that I wouldn't have taken her hand.

She pivoted, and like an eager little puppy, I followed her across the living room, past the small kitchen, and into the bedroom on the other side of the suite. I pushed the door closed behind us, and Evin turned, appraising my cluttered, temporary space.

"You're messy?" she asked, and although I couldn't see her, I heard the smile in her voice.

I shrugged and kicked one of my suitcases closed. "Sometimes. When I'm traveling? Yes. But this had more to do with trying to get changed out of my airport outfit in time to come impress you."

Still holding my hand, she spun around. "I'm very easy to impress, Lucy. You could have shown up in a paper bag, and I still would've been captivated by you."

I closed the short distance between us and dropped my hands to her waist. "Is that so?"

"Yes," she confirmed quickly, clasping her hands against my cheeks. "You're gorgeous, but I'm sure you're used to hearing that."

My eyes bounced between hers, and I followed the line of her slightly tilted lips. Like we couldn't stand the very minute amount of room between us, we moved closer still.

"Sure, but it means so much more coming from you."

Her smile widened as she slanted her mouth over mine, which made for an awkward kiss that we ended up laughing through.

"On the bed," she said. "I want you on the bed." She walked backward, and I shuffled forward, willing to do whatever she wanted as long as she kept kissing me and touching me.

She turned, and I felt the edge of the bed behind me. She pushed my shoulders lightly, and I dropped down onto it, reluctantly letting her lips go. My hands swept down her legs and braced around the back of her thighs.

She stepped between my legs, and I looked up at her as she pushed my hair behind my shoulders and brushed her fingers down the side of my neck.

"I want..." she said again as she had in the living room only moments earlier. Similarly, her words trailed off. I noted the hesitation in her eyes and the way she chewed on her lower lip.

"Tell me, Evin. I want to hear what *you* want."

She swallowed and took a deep breath as I squeezed her legs.

"I want to...taste you."

I couldn't help it—my eyes fluttered shut, and I moaned just at the thought of her face between my thighs.

"But I've never done it before," she quickly added. "So, don't get your hopes up. I could be horrible at it."

"You won't be," I said with unwavering confidence. Anything she did to me, I would love and ask for more. "Just think about what you like and do that."

"But—" she began again, and I shook my head.

"I'll talk you through it if I need to. I'm really not worried, Evin. Now, either hurry up and get your mouth on me or take my spot on the bed so I can taste you."

My pulse raced, and my desire was sitting heavy and low in my stomach. It felt like it was racing through my veins and simmering beneath my skin. Hell, I was two seconds away from asking if I could ride *her* thigh.

But she straightened before I could suggest any alternatives and reached for the bottom of my top. I lifted my hands over my head, and she tugged it off before tossing it on the ground beside us.

Her eyes immediately dropped to my chest and my basic

black bra. She reached forward and ran her fingers over my collarbones, then dropped them lower and lower until she traced the top of the fabric.

She'd barely touched me, yet it was unlike anything I'd ever felt before. She touched me like no one else had, and no one else probably would.

Then she kissed me—*hard*—and pressed me back into the bed. She guided me backward, and I willingly went until my head hit the pillows and she was poised above me.

My legs fell open, and she kissed down my neck. Placing warm, open-mouth kisses over my skin, I squirmed beneath her, hoping she would touch me more. Her lips brushed the center of my chest. I opened my eyes in time to see her shaking hand grasp my breast, but I didn't say anything. Because the second she touched me, her hand was steady and sure.

She tugged the cup down and massaged my breast. It felt so good, but it felt even better when she dropped her mouth onto my nipple and slipped her tongue around it.

"Yes, *yes*," I chanted. My fingers weaved through her hair as I carefully held her against me. She circled the hard point, easily gliding her tongue around and around, teasing the crap out of me and amplifying my desire with every pass.

My broken cry tapered off into a moan when she sucked hard enough that my fingers dug into her scalp and my other hand grappled for her. She switched to my other breast and repeated the same pattern. Licking and sucking my nipple, her hands wandered lower until she teased the top of my skirt.

Wanting so badly to feel more of her, wanting her to touch me everywhere, I helped by lifting my hips and reaching behind me to unzip my skirt. Together, we pushed it down my legs, and Evin tossed it away as she had my shirt.

Left only in my bra—with the cups pushed down—my matching plain, black panties, and tights, there wasn't much left for the imagination. Evin's hazel eyes raked up and down my body, and I shivered under her gaze.

She licked her lips and gripped my waist, running her thumb back and forth where the top of my tights began.

"You're like a dream," she muttered, reaching forward to slip my tights off as well. She kissed my legs as she went, pulling them down and brushing her lips against my newly exposed skin.

"Your mouth feels like a dream," I muttered as she looked back up at me.

Her hands massaged up the inside of my thighs, and my legs fell back open. The cooler air hit my soaked panties, and I fisted the sheets beneath me.

Evin stared between my legs like she was both intimidated and enthralled. Similar to how I imagined I looked during my first experience with a woman—how many people are during their first sexual experience with any person.

But she licked her lips, and I watched all the hesitation burn away with unmistakable hunger taking its place.

Pushing up until I was seated before her, I tugged the sleeves of her dress down her arms. Watching her watch me, I suddenly realized she was way too overdressed. She freed her arms and readjusted between my legs so I could finish undressing her.

I slipped the dress off and dropped it on the floor. I muttered a curse under my breath as my eyes raked over her, realizing that her bra matched her light pink panties. She looked like a sweet, little angel in front of me.

Except she was anything but. She pushed against my shoulders until I was lying flat on the bed once again. Then she forced my legs open with her hands against my inner thighs. Her nails dug into my skin, and I took a deep breath.

"You're incredible, Lucy. Every part of you is...*incredible*," she said on a sigh, sitting back on her heels and massaging her way up my legs. My heart raced, and she stopped only when the tips of her thumbs teased the edge of my underwear.

twelve

. . .

Lucy

FINALLY, she licked her lips and ran her finger over the thin fabric covering my pussy. I sucked in a sharp breath, and her eyes flicked to mine as she did it again. When she swiped against my clit, just the smallest touch made pleasure spear through me.

She watched my reactions and sucked in a shaky breath.

Lifting her hands, she slipped her fingers beneath the fabric at my hips and dragged them down my legs. She did so slowly, so fucking slowly that I was shaking in anticipation. She tossed them to the side—I didn't see where—and set her attention back between my legs.

I let them fall open, and the cool air hit my wet skin.

"Fuck," she muttered under her breath. She reached her hands forward, and I sucked in a steadying breath as she touched my bare skin. Her thumbs traced down my lips and spread me open. "You're already so wet."

I moaned as the pad of her thumb connected with my clit. "Because I've been thinking about this—about you—for weeks. And being around you all night—" I gasped when her thumb continued lower, sweeping over my opening and through my arousal. "And watching you come all over my thigh was so fucking hot."

"It was hot," she murmured. She lifted her hand to her mouth and dragged the pad of her thumb against her tongue before replacing it against my pulsing, swollen point. The tiny, firm circles made my hips jolt to meet her hand, and sweeping, unending pleasure took hold of me.

She stared between my legs with her jaw slack and her soft skin glowing in the faint light of the lamps scattered about the room. And she was more than I could have dreamed up. It was a lot of pressure to be her first experience with a woman, but I also wouldn't have traded it for the world.

The look of wonder on her face was genuine and only magnified every sensation.

I closed my eyes and focused on the way she touched me— on the urgent movement of her thumb and the gentle pressure of her other hand on my thigh. Her sweet, soft breaths dotted the air around us and mingled with my own.

I was desperate when her thumb disappeared, but my disappointment lasted only as long as it took for her to stroke my entrance. My eyes flew open, and her attention bounced to my face.

There was a lingering hesitation behind her hazel eyes that I read immediately. Through clenched teeth and a sharp breath, I nodded. She took my silent answer for exactly what it was: a plea to keep going.

Thankfully, she didn't wait another second. With our eyes locked, she slowly pushed her finger inside me. My gasp was inadvertent, as was the way I clenched around her finger. She paused for a moment, and I could feel the flush climbing up my chest and neck.

When I was about to beg her to keep moving, she began testing it—dragging her finger in and out of me and finding my G-spot with skillful ease. My desire was wound so tight, I couldn't help but cant my hips in time with her. She found the perfect rhythm, then added a second finger.

"Yes, yes," I gasped as my orgasm wound tight in my lower stomach, and I clenched around her fingers. My eyes had slipped closed, overwhelmed by each sensation and newly confident stroke of her fingers. If she hadn't told me earlier that she'd never done anything like this before, I would have thought she was a pro.

She absolutely knew what she was doing, as was evidenced by the wetness between my legs that was growing with every intentional sweep of her fingers.

"Evin," I moaned. "That's so good."

"Your body is telling me as much," she murmured, and even with my eyes closed, I could hear the smile in her voice.

My lips tilted up until she ground another finger against my clit, and my smile dropped so I could let out a guttural growl. "Yes, just like that. Such a good girl. You're going to make me come."

"No." Evin's response was so abrupt, my eyes popped open. She looked like a sweet, sultry angel poised between my legs in her pink bra and panties, but her face was serious and masked in need.

She slowly pulled her fingers free and lifted them to her mouth, slipping them against her tongue and closing her lips around them. She sucked the taste of me as her eyes fluttered shut and she moaned quietly.

My entire body was on fire watching her enjoy the taste of me. Like every nerve ending was alive and primed for more.

She dropped her eyes back to me, then slid back until she was on her stomach between my spread legs. It happened so fast, I was surprised by the feeling of her hot breath against my wet slit.

"You can't come until I've tasted you," she clarified. She propped herself on her elbows and ran her fingers along my lower lips, spreading me apart and exposing my damp skin to the cooler air.

"It won't take very long," I confessed. Actually, even that may have been a bit of a lie—I didn't know if I would last more than a minute.

She hummed and lowered her face until she was eye level with my cunt. My entire body tensed in rapt anticipation.

"I just want it to be good," she admitted. "I like to be good at things."

I smiled softly at her honesty and reached forward, letting my hands run through her brown locks and drop down her cheek.

"I'm not worried, Evin. Everything you've done thus far has been...better."

"Better?"

I nodded and forced myself to swallow before I continued. "Better than anything has been before."

thirteen

. . .

Evin

LUCY'S HONESTY did wonders to put my nerves at ease. And I couldn't wait another second to know what she tasted like or how her perfect pussy felt against my tongue.

Licking her arousal on my fingers was only a tease. I needed it straight from the source.

Dipping my head lower, I held her open with my fingers and pressed one soft kiss to her clit. She gasped and ground her hips like she was searching for more, which I took as my cue to keep going. I kissed her again, only the second time, I let my tongue slip out and flick across her pulsing point.

A louder gasp was followed by a moan, and hell, I was already addicted to eliciting those reactions from her. I wanted more.

I flattened my tongue and moved lower, licking her opening up to her clit. She tasted just as good as I knew she would—sweet and slightly earthy—and I couldn't get enough. Ignoring all the questions and insecurities, I pushed them to the back of my mind and let my instincts guide me. What I liked—that's what Lucy said I should do to her. But with each swipe of my tongue, I learned what she liked, too.

I wrapped one under her thigh and tugged her closer, flattening my palm against her soft skin. With my free hand, I slipped my fingers between my mouth and her body, replacing them inside her wet heat.

God, she felt so good. So soft and wet, she greedily clamped down around my finger. I wasn't sure how I'd gone twenty-eight years without this, but I knew I never would again.

It took me several seconds to find the right combination—I was good at multitasking but learning how to move my fingers against her G-spot and flick my tongue over her clit was something all new. Still, she grew wetter, her arousal collecting around my fingers and making the most beautifully obscene sound with every movement. They mingled with her deep, sultry moans, creating the most intoxicating melody I'd ever heard.

Her body was warm against mine as I flattened my tongue against her clit and added pressure. She cried out and slipped her hand in the back of my hair, nails scraping against my scalp and sending a shiver down my spine.

I looked up her body and found her eyes locked on where I was settled between her legs. Her wet, plump lips were parted, and her skin was flushed, each breath coming out in a short pant.

"That feels so good," she said quickly. "Oh my god, Evin. I'm almost—"

Her words cut off abruptly, but I knew what she was about to say. I could feel her orgasm bearing down on her in the way her body tensed and she squeezed my fingers.

I redoubled my efforts, fucking her with my fingers and pressing my tongue harder against her pulsing clit. She chanted "yes, yes, yes" as her hand tightened in my hair and her thighs flexed.

Her orgasm flooded my fingers and my tongue as a feeling of

triumph washed over me. I peered up her body once again to watch the ecstasy cross her face, and I could have watched it forever. I swore I would watch it over and over again. I had to.

She bucked against my face, and I held on as she cried out, her back bowing with the power of it. She'd barely come down from her high when she leaned forward and urged me up. I crawled over her, and she clasped her hands on either side of my face, slamming her mouth to mine and tasting herself on my tongue.

The kiss was carnal and heated. Her hands ran down my back and skillfully undid my bra. I let fabric fall down my arms and tossed it to the side. Lucy's hands were immediately against my breasts, her thumbs circling my nipples and pinching them until they were hard points.

God, I was so wet, and I wanted her hands everywhere all at once. I found myself grinding my hips against her thigh like I had earlier, but the friction of my wet panties wasn't enough.

In the next second, Lucy shifted and flipped us until she was poised on top of me. With one final brush of her tongue against mine, she moved her mouth over my neck and down my chest. She pushed my breasts together and sucked one nipple into her mouth. My entire body lit up with pleasure.

She swapped to the other breast and ran her tongue around the point, flicking against me in a way that belied all the dirty and skilled things she could do with it.

"You're so beautiful, Evin," she murmured against my skin. Her hands slipped down my sides, and she continued her very intent descent down my body. "I'm going to spend all night kissing and touching every inch of you."

She slipped her fingers beneath my panties and dragged them down my legs without delay. "But there's one very important part of your body I need to touch and kiss first. I feel like I'm going to go crazy if I don't," she said, pushing my legs open and guiding her fingers through my trimmed, dark curls and against my bare lips.

"We wouldn't want that," I said through a gasp. She circled my clit with her thumb and pushed two fingers inside me. Our eyes connected, and a wickedly beautiful grin curved her lips.

I took another breath, and she was suddenly on her stomach and poised between my legs. I didn't have a chance to prepare myself before her mouth was on me. She moaned against me as she lapped at my cunt, and I could feel the vibration of her moan throughout my entire body.

As I expected, her tongue was just as adept as her fingers. Tasting her and touching her already had me temptingly close to the edge, my desire churning and sweeping inside me. So when her tongue met my damp flesh, I knew it would be mere seconds, maybe a minute or two, before I was flying over the edge.

The pads of her fingers scraped my inner walls and peppered my pussy with open-mouth kisses, letting her tongue linger and lap at every inch of me.

My fingers gripped the sheets beneath me, and I ground my teeth together.

"Come for me, baby," she muttered against my skin. Her fingers pushed into me harder as she sucked my clit between her lips.

And everything around me exploded. Like energy arching between us, the orgasm shot through me. I'd never been so consumed by a release before. So utterly rocked that every after-shock was like another zap to my system.

Lucy rode it out with me, keeping her fingers buried between my legs and her tongue against my flesh. I rode her face and nearly screamed, but I was beyond caring who heard. I just wanted to relish that feeling forever.

"There we go," Lucy murmured. "Such a good girl. So pretty when you come for me."

One final wave, and my body was spent. I dropped back onto the bed and tried to slow my pulse and catch my breath.

The bed dipped around me, and Lucy was above me once

again. I slowly opened my eyes to find her smiling down at me. She pressed her lips to mine, but when she tried to pull away, I clasped her cheeks and kept her there. I wanted to taste myself on her mouth, on her sweet lips.

Unlike before, our kiss was unhurried. She settled next to me and draped my thigh over her legs. Her arm slipped beneath my head, and we lay there for a while, kissing and touching and laughing. There wasn't any intention behind it besides to feel one another, to learn the other's body.

And she felt so good against me. Lucy nipped at my bottom lip, and I sat back, trying to swallow the very girly giggle climbing up my throat.

"I'm so…" I began, but my words trailed off.

"Satisfied?" Lucy tried with a smile, sweeping a stray piece of hair from my face and tucking it behind my ear.

I laughed and trailed my fingers between her breasts. "Yes, but I was going to say, happy."

"Me, too," she whispered. Our noses brushed, and I sighed. A deep contentment descended over me as I breathed her in. It felt good—*so* good.

My phone vibrated on the bedside table, and Lucy laughed. "You should probably check that."

I huffed out a breath, not wanting to pop our bubble, but knowing she was right. It had vibrated several times in the past few minutes, and I assumed it was Aiden. I'd promised to check in, which I'm usually good at, but I was too caught up in Lucy that I'd forgotten.

I retrieved my phone before I rolled back into Lucy and unlocked it. As I suspected, there were a few missed texts from Aiden.

> Aiden: Let me know you're okay. I'm guessing you are since you're at some fancy hotel downtown?

The messages following the text were photos of Aiden and a

few of our other friends. I could tell from the background that they were at our favorite bar not too far away.

"He knows you're here?" Lucy said, looking over my shoulder.

I nodded and sent a quick text letting him know I was more than okay and to have fun.

"Yeah, he has my location on his phone, so he probably checked where I was when I didn't respond. It's our way of keeping track of each other just in case. Especially since we're both dating."

"That's smart," she agreed. "I never thought about that."

"I guess your life probably looks a little different than ours, so I'm not surprised."

She chuckled as I dropped my phone onto the bed and focused my attention back on her.

"A little would be putting it mildly. Honestly, I didn't even consider sharing location. I don't think I've been truly alone in… forever. There's no reason for someone to watch my location anyway."

There was a slight sadness in her voice, barely noticeable but still there all the same. It made my heart hurt hearing it.

"We're alone right now," I said, and she offered me a small smile.

"It's all an illusion. We're alone in here, but there is security stationed at the door, and if I wanted to leave, they'd be with me, too. Like going to the bar with Aiden and your other friends. That would never happen. We'd have to find a private room and additional security just in case."

"You hate it?"

She shrugged. "It's a part of the job. A very necessary part if I want to keep doing my job, which I do. It's just moments like these when I get a little…irritated with it. With all of it."

"Moments like these?" I asked, tracing the curve of her shoulder and trailing my fingers down her arm, which rested on my hip. Her eyes met mine, and the green of her irises was stark and bright.

She lifted her hand and cupped the side of my neck, tracing my jaw with her thumb.

"When I'm thinking about the future and what that might look like for me. And for...someone else. What they'd have to put up with to be with me."

"Hmm," I hummed in understanding. Being with Lucy would look much different than being with anyone else. Her job and her fame would always be the third and fourth people in any relationship—that much was easy to surmise. Everyone else would want a piece of her, too, but she was just one person.

I didn't know exactly what she was thinking about the future, but I hoped she was considering one with me. It felt insane since we'd only been texting for a few months and had just met in person, but I wanted that. It felt a shame not to try at the very least. It was too good with her—better than good, really—and I wanted more.

"I think it would be worth it," I said honestly. Her attention bounced from my lips to my eyes, and I noted the surprise behind them. "You are worth it."

Her surprise faded, and a slow smile tilted her lips. She leaned forward and kissed me thoroughly. When she pulled back, I was breathless, and my heart had started pounding in my chest.

"You say things like that, and it just makes me like you more, Evin. I didn't think it was possible."

"I think this goes without saying, but I like you, too, Lucy. So much."

She kissed me again, and I savored every sweep of her tongue and caress of her lips. I let my hands wander, and she did the same. Eventually, we slipped between the clean sheets and lost ourselves in each other once again.

fourteen

...

Evin

When I woke up the next morning, I could feel Lucy next to me. She was starfished on her side of the bed, and I had starfished partially on top of her. My body was sore in the best way.

I didn't remember what time we'd gone to sleep, but it had been extraordinarily late—or really early, depending on how you thought about it. And although I was exhausted, I didn't regret one single moment, and I wanted to do anything but move. I buried my nose into her hair and took a deep breath, willing sleep to take me again.

Until there was a loud pounding on the bedroom door. My eyes flew open, and I tensed.

"Lucy!" someone yelled and knocked again. "Honey, you have to get up!"

Lucy stirred with a groan and buried her face deeper into the pillows beneath her. A second later, her alarm went off, and she blindly reached for it, smacking at the screen of her phone until it shut off.

I rolled away from her and onto my back, blinking away the lingering sleep in my eyes.

The person on the other side of the door shouted her name one more time. "Please answer if you're awake, you have a meeting in—"

"Yes, I'm awake," Lucy said. "Thank you."

I cringed and immediately felt weird that I'd stayed. Like I was interrupting or in the middle of her busy day and making it harder for everyone else as well.

I grabbed the edge of the sheets and contemplated rolling out of bed when Lucy turned toward me with a sleepy, sincere smile.

"Morning," she said, sleep still heavy in her voice. She laid her head down on my pillow and tugged me closer with an arm around my waist. Her black hair fanned around us, and I scooted closer until our noses brushed and I could enjoy her warmth.

"Morning."

She kissed me softly, and as much as I loved her lips on mine, I was self-conscious about my morning breath. Lucy didn't seem to have the same issue, though. She slipped her arm beneath me and tightened her hold until our naked bodies were pressed together, and all I could see and feel was her.

"You're going to New York, right?" I asked, and she sighed against my mouth.

"Yeah," she said dejectedly.

Her mood shifted in an instant, and her eyes dropped to where her hand lingered against my chest.

"I've never been, but I've always wanted to go."

"I wish you could come with me," she said. And I wished I could, too. But I couldn't just up and leave—I had work and plans with my family. "It would be so much better with you there."

I gave her a soft smile and kissed her again. But we couldn't linger too long. Voices echoed from the living room, and our bubble I'd been so fond of was well and truly gone.

"We should probably get up. Madison will be back soon with the cavalry if I don't go out there."

Like neither of us wanted to, but still knew we should, we lingered in each other's arms until the noise in the living room grew to a volume we couldn't ignore. Begrudgingly, we both rolled out of bed, and I quickly found my dress and other clothes on the floor.

"Do you want the bathroom first?" Lucy asked, and I shook my head, waving for her to go ahead.

While she was in there, I got dressed. It felt strange to put on the same clothes as last night, but I didn't have anything else. While I was zipping my dress, I spotted one of my books. Lucy's copy she wanted me to sign specifically for her.

I crossed to her dresser and flipped through the well-worn copy. The creased pages made me smile, and I realized in that moment exactly what I wanted to write inside it. I grabbed the pen found in every hotel room and wrote quickly on the title page. It was a bold message. One that made my feelings and intentions obvious, but I did it anyway.

I dropped the pen and closed the book only a second before Lucy returned.

I walked past her and into the bathroom.

When I came back, she was dressed, too. She wore a pair of light-wash jeans and a plain white tee. She'd swept her dark hair into a bun on top of her head, and my first thought was how stunning she was. No matter what she wore or how little sleep she'd gotten, she was breathtaking.

She caught me staring and walked over to me. She took one of my hands, and I willingly stepped into her embrace. We held each other for a moment, and I wanted to extend that moment forever. I would have if I could, but eventually we stepped back.

With her hands against my cheeks, Lucy took a deep breath. "I don't want this to be the last time I see you, Evin. It can't be."

"It won't," I said immediately. "We'll figure it out. I want to see you again. Whenever you can."

"It might not be for a while." Although I figured that would be the case, my heart ached at the confirmation. The reality appeared to hit us both at the same time as we stood there. We lived completely different lives in different states. Long distance was hard enough when one person wasn't already a famous actor that couldn't go anywhere—not even the grocery store—without being recognized.

But even with all the reasons why it likely wouldn't work, I still couldn't let her go completely. I had faith. In us and in what we were together, even in such a short time.

I took a deep breath. "Whenever you can, then, I'll be here."

"I can't make you promise that, Evin. It's not fair to you."

I shook my head and covered her hands still against my face. I laced our fingers together and mustered a smile that I knew didn't meet my eyes. "You're not making me do anything, Lucy. You're worth it, remember?"

Tears welled in her eyes, and everything within me urged me to make them disappear. I leaned forward and was rudely interrupted by the blonde woman I now knew as Madison stepping through the door.

She stopped the moment she saw us, eyes widening as she cleared her throat. She looked appropriately embarrassed and apologetic.

"I'm so sorry, but Evin, I have a car waiting for you downstairs to take you home. Lucy, we have to leave for the airport in half an hour."

I didn't wait for Lucy to say anything. I stepped out of her hold and nodded to Madison.

"Let me just grab my shoes and purse," I said, motioning to the living room behind her. She let me pass, and I found them exactly where I'd left them, as well as about four other people milling about.

I was a little embarrassed, which only made me move faster and refuse to look anyone in the eye. I tugged on my shoes and grabbed my bag, making my way to the door where Lucy was standing.

Madison pulled it open for me, but I lingered for a moment,

staring at Lucy. I wanted one last goodbye. One last kiss, but I didn't know if she wanted to show that type of affection—or any affection—in front of everyone around us.

So, instead, I gave her a soft smile and a small wave before I stepped out into the hallway, where I was greeted by two security guards.

"Right this way, Ms. Morgan."

"Wait." Lucy spoke up from behind me. I whirled as she stepped into the doorway. One hand was at my neck, and the other was around my waist as she tugged me into a kiss. A knee-weakening, life-changing kiss that made everything and everyone else around us vanish.

It was all too quick, but I was glad it had happened anyway. Hopefully it would be enough to last me until I saw her again. Although I knew it likely wouldn't.

fifteen

. . .

Lucy

> Evin: I still smell like you.

MY HEART DID a weird stuttering skip when I read the text. Already in my seat on the plane, I tried to hide my smile as the rest of my team and security filed on.

It had only been a little over an hour since I'd left Evin, and it took everything in me to let her go rather than ask that she drop everything and come with me. I worried that she would see the complexity of being with someone like me when I left and think better of it.

But I'd asked that she text me when she got home, and she had. That had done a lot to calm my nerves.

> Me: And I still smell like you. I didn't even want to brush my teeth this morning so I could taste you a little while longer.

> Evin: But you did, right? Oral health is very important.

I threw my hand over my mouth to stifle my laugh. Madison, who was concerned about Evin, gave me a worried look from her seat just ahead of me.

But I didn't care. I knew it was her job to worry, and once she got to know Evin better, she'd learn there was nothing to worry about.

One night with Evin was never going to be enough. I needed her like I needed air in my lungs, which was a jarring, eye-opening realization.

I would do anything to make it work—to make *us* work. Although we hadn't said anything definitive, it was only a matter of time before I remedied that. I had to get through the rest of the press tour, and I would have a few weeks off, which I wanted to spend in Dallas with her.

It would work out; I had to believe it would, otherwise I was bound to spiral.

Me: Yes, I brushed my teeth.

Evin: Good. I promise it won't be the last time you have the taste of me on your tongue anyway. ;)

I glanced out the window and shook my head, swallowing down my groan.

Me: Then we're in agreement. I can't wait for that to happen.

Evin: Me neither. You know where to find me whenever you're free.

I was typing out a response when the attendant stepped forward and cleared her throat. We all looked up at her. She appeared nervous, wringing her hands together in front of her and nibbling her lower lip.

"I'm so sorry, Ms. Lowe, but it appears the Wi-Fi on the plane is down. If you want to deboard, we can try to get you a new aircraft, but I'm not sure how long—"

I waved her off with a smile, trying to stop her nervous rambling and put her at ease.

"It's not a big deal," I said. "We can all spend a few hours without our phones. It's not the end of the world."

We didn't have time to wait for a new plane, and I was right —a little over three hours wouldn't kill anyone.

> Me: We're about to take off and don't have any Wi-Fi on the plane. I'll text you when we land.

> Evin: Have a safe flight!

I locked my phone and stared out the window as we began to taxi. Soon I'd be even farther away from Evin, and my heart sank.

It was possibly the longest flight of my life. The moment we landed, and I got a signal again, I texted Evin.

She'd responded quickly and told me she'd been writing while I was in the air. As someone who now cared about her, I loved that she was doing what she loved, but as a fan of her work, I also couldn't wait to read it.

We went straight from the airport to the hotel, where I spent all of an hour before we went directly to the set of the show. Late-night shows weren't too hard. I knew they would lean into the lighter topics, and even if we did broach deeper subjects, Simon—the host—wouldn't push too far.

Sitting in the chair, I stared into the mirror as my hair and makeup artists got to work making me TV-ready. We had already done some promo, so they were only doing a few final touches to make sure I was perfect for the pre-taped interview. We were going for a smart, sleek look—slicking my hair back into a ponytail with long lashes and a red lip. I was also extremely excited about the outfit my stylist had selected—a black pantsuit and a white button-down top that showed a decent amount of cleavage.

Simon had already visited my dressing room to discuss the topics he wanted to bring up. We were going to talk about the movie, of course, as well as Evin, but only so much that she was my favorite author and the impact my posts had on her career.

I agreed that I'd be open to discussing it all, even though I had to tamp down my reaction when he said Evin's name. While they finished up my makeup and my hair, I tapped my hands nervously against my thighs.

Madison had taken my phone to hold so I could pay attention to the social media promo stuff and pre-interviews, but she'd done so earlier than necessary. She made some excuse about me needing to focus and grabbed it up before I could argue. Then she'd run off while I was still stuck in the chair the first time around.

My makeup and hair team instructed me to get dressed again, which I did carefully without messing up their beautiful work. I buttoned up the low-cut top and threw on the blazer. With the matching red heels, I felt powerful, unstoppable.

I was looking in the mirror, feeling the usual nerves knowing I was about to be on TV, when Madison came rushing into the room.

"Lucy," she said, and I could tell by the look on her face that something was wrong. Immediately my thoughts jumped to the worst possible conclusion—something had happened to Evin or my family.

Thankfully, she didn't leave me in suspense for long.

"I—I didn't know whether I should tell you this or not, but... pictures of you were posted online. News sites are picking them up, and pretty soon they'll be everywhere."

My panic subsided and was immediately replaced with frustration. "Pictures are posted of me all the time. I don't know why you're—"

With a few quick steps, she stopped in front of me and held

out her phone. My heart dropped into my stomach which churned.

The first photo was of Evin and me at dinner. Through the small opening in the curtains, someone had taken a photo of us at the table. Evin's head was tilted back in laughter, and I was staring at her like she was my entire world. There was another of us at the table once again, but it was tame—nothing out of the ordinary except two friends having dinner.

The third photo took my breath away. Someone had managed to make their way up to the penthouse level and caught the moment I'd kissed Evin that morning outside of my room. There was no denying who we were or what we were doing.

I scrolled back up and read the headline and started skimming from the beginning of the article.

Just a fan? Lucy Lowe's Secret Girlfriend and Favorite Author

The article incorrectly surmised that my relationship with Evin had started long before the first interview when I'd mentioned her book. And what broke my heart even more was that they hypothesized I'd only recommended her books because she was my girlfriend.

"Oh my god," I muttered, my hand shaking as I gave Madison her phone back.

"I've already spoken to Simon's team, and unfortunately, he wants to discuss the photos. But I can put my foot down. I can threaten to walk if he doesn't agree not to bring them up."

I shook my head. Even through the anger, I was formulating a plan. "No," I said quickly, and Madison looked at me, completely stunned.

"Lucy, you can't—"

"I can. I'm going to fix this; I *have* to fix this." Then it dawned on me. "She hasn't even come out to her parents yet. Those fuckers have outed her to the entire world. I want to find the person who did this and—"

"Yes, I promise, we're on it, Lucy. But I can't let you go out there without any preparation."

"You can, and you will. I will be fine. I've had years of media training exactly for moments like this. And whether Simon wants to talk about Evin or not, he won't push me too hard. We have a good friendship, and I trust that it won't be a bloodbath."

Madison sighed and ran her hand through her usually perfectly styled blonde hair. She dropped her head back and groaned toward the ceiling. When she looked back at me, she looked like she was contemplating whether she wanted to argue further. But with another dejected breath, she nodded.

"Fine, but I don't love this," she said. "For the record."

"I understand, and I appreciate that. Now, I need my phone so I can call Evin."

Done fighting me, Madison reached into her pocket and handed me my phone. There was a missed text from Evin from our earlier conversation, but nothing newer, which meant she might not have seen the photos yet. I could only hope.

I went to tap her name when an assistant knocked on the door.

"Two-minute warning," she said. "I'm here to walk you down, Ms. Lowe."

"Fuck," I muttered under my breath. I didn't have time to call her. Without another option, I sent the quickest text I could.

> Me: I'm about to go on. I'm so sorry about the photos. I'm going to fix this.

I handed Madison back my phone and turned to look in the mirror one final time. But my eyes snagged on the book sitting on the counter instead. It was the first copy of one of Evin's books I'd purchased. The one she hadn't found time to sign since we were otherwise occupied. Still, it was comforting to flip through the pages quickly. Seeing her words did more than I realized they would to settle my nerves.

And right as I was going to put it down, I saw the words on the title page. She had signed it, and the note made me want to cry and scream and fly back to her right then.

To Lucy (my #1 fan),

The greatest story hasn't been written yet, because I think it might be ours.

xo

Evin

sixteen

. . .

Evin

LOST IN MY STORY, I looked up and scrubbed my eyes. Aiden would be over any second with a late-night snack and drinks so we could watch Lucy's late show appearance together. We'd taken bets earlier about whether they'd bring me up. He guaranteed they would, and I would have rather they not.

Picking up my phone to check Aiden's location, I unlocked the screen the same second my mom began calling me.

I glanced at the clock before I answered. It was almost ten thirty, which was much later than she was usually awake. I'd also spent a good amount of time with them earlier in the day, so I wasn't sure why she would be calling me.

"Hello?" I said, answering quickly and not doing very well to mask the concern in my voice.

"Hey, sweet girl. How's it goin'?" My mom's southern drawl sounded like home, but even in her few words, I could hear something hidden behind them.

"It's going fine, Mom. How about you?"

My question was met with silence. A loaded silence that made my heart beat faster.

"Mom? What's wrong?" I asked. I wasn't going to wait for her to tell me on her own. Knowing her, it might be several minutes of forced pleasantries and standard catching-up questions before she got to the point, and my anxiety couldn't handle that right then.

"Geez, Evin. I didn't know if this was the best way to handle it or if we should just wait until you said something."

My pulse was racing, and my palms were sweating as I clutched the phone to my ear.

"Okay, you're scaring me now. Can you please just tell me?"

With a long, deep sigh, she finally spoke. "Have you been on social media recently? There's a photo of you...and Lucy Lowe."

Shit, shit, shit, I thought. I hoped this wouldn't happen, but spending time with Lucy in public, I knew it was a possibility.

"I've been writing, so my phone was on silent for a few hours. Photos from dinner? We umm...she came to my signing yesterday, and we had dinner afterward. I told you about that."

"Yes, you did," she said. "And I still think it's so great that she surprised you, but..." There was still a slight waver in her words, so I held my breath as she continued. "But this photo looks like it was taken outside a hotel room."

"What?" I managed to ask through my shock and disbelief.

"Okay, so you haven't seen it?"

"No, umm...one second."

I immediately put her on speakerphone and started searching with shaking fingers. I tapped on the first result, and three photos popped up. Two of us at dinner and one of us outside her hotel room when she'd kissed me before I left.

Tears welled in my eyes, and I drew in a shaky breath. Now, it wasn't just my hands that were shaking. My entire body shuddered, and I had the sudden, violent urge to puke.

"Evin?" My mom's voice broke through my panic, and I took her off speakerphone, pressing the phone to my ear.

"Yeah," I said with a deep breath.

"You know we don't care, right? Your dad and I love you no

matter *who* you love. It doesn't change a damn thing. And I'm sorry you didn't feel like you could tell us."

The tears began to fall, and I looked across my little studio apartment to see Aiden pushing through my front door. He was carrying bags of supplies and immediately spotted me across the room.

He dropped the bags and crossed to me, pointing to the phone and mouthing, *"Who's that?"*

"My mom," I mouthed back and gave him a thumbs-up. He nodded but still wrapped me in a hug, which only made me cry harder.

"Oh, sweet girl," my mom said when Aiden let me go.

"I'm okay," I said. "And it's something I've only recently learned about myself. I was going to tell you both soon. I just wanted to come to terms with it myself first."

"I understand. We all understand, honey."

I took a deep breath and watched Aiden unload the bags of food and drinks onto my kitchen counter. I was happy he was there.

"I'm sorry you had to find out about it this way."

She tsked, and I imagined her dramatically waving off my apology. "You have nothing to be sorry about. If anything, *I'm* sorry that it happened this way."

"Yeah, me too," I agreed.

"Anyway, we love you so much, Evin. Call me whenever and we can talk some more, okay? Or maybe come by sometime this week."

"I will, Mom. Love you."

I hung up and set my phone onto the counter, resting my arms on the cold granite and dropping my head on top of them. I groaned in frustration so I wouldn't keep crying.

"Have you seen them?" I asked Aiden without lifting my head.

He was quiet for a moment, but he finally spoke. "Yeah."

Not usually a man of few words, I looked up to find him

pointedly not looking at me and rearranging the already organized food.

"What is it? What are people saying?"

I reached for my phone, but his hand landed on top of mine. He shook his head, and dread fell over me.

"You don't want to read any of those articles or anything else."

"Then tell me. I can't not know, Aiden."

He rolled his lips and braced his hands on the counter in front of him.

"They're assuming that you and Lucy started a relationship prior to her first interview, meaning that she only mentioned your book because you were sleeping together. And that—"

"Her endorsement was disingenuous," I finished for him.

Aiden shrugged. "Essentially."

With another groan, I had no idea what to do. All I knew was that I needed to talk to Lucy. I wanted to hear from her.

But there was already a missed text from her. It was sent several hours before. Right when I'd turned my phone off and zoned in on my writing.

"Lucy said she's going to fix it," I said, reading the short message for the third time. If I'd known my world was going to turn upside down, I would have had my phone on. But she'd warned me that she wouldn't be accessible most of the day. That the interview wasn't the only commitment she had, and she'd call or text me later that night.

"How?" he asked, and I shook my head.

Pushing away from the counter, I jogged into my little living room and turned on the TV. I'd gotten a free trial of a live TV service just for this interview, and I'd planned to add the expense into my budget for any future interviews.

"I don't know, but she's about to be on."

Aiden came to sit down beside me with a glass containing a clear liquid and ice. I took a large sip, which was a horrible idea.

My face screwed up as the liquor burned a path down my throat. "That's straight tequila," I choked out.

"It felt necessary."

And he was right. I was shaking with anticipation when the host stepped from around his desk and waved toward the opposite side of the stage. "Please welcome the incomparable Lucy Lowe!"

seventeen

. . .

Evin

LUCY STEPPED ONTO THE STAGE, and I sucked in a sharp breath.

"Fuck, she's gorgeous," Aiden said next to me, and all I could do was nod.

The most beautiful woman on the planet—I'd seen so many similar headlines and always agreed. But knowing her personally and understanding the genuinely good person she was made it even more true.

Her black suit was perfectly tailored to show off her curves and long legs, as was the white shirt beneath it, which displayed her cleavage tastefully. Her hair was slicked back in a kick-ass ponytail, and her red lips were kissable. I bit mine with the reminder of what they felt like and blushed when the memories flooded back in.

Like everything was perfectly fine, Lucy smiled and waved to the crowd as she walked across the stage. She greeted Simon with a hug and waved to the audience one last time before she sat in the chair closest to his desk.

Simon clapped and smiled at her. "Welcome back, Lucy. It's been, what? A year at least?"

She nodded and crossed her legs. "I think it has been. You missed me, didn't you, Simon?"

Simon laughed, and away they went. Aiden reached for my hand, and I willingly took it, squeezing it tightly and resting our joined hands on my thigh. I appreciated his unwavering support. Ever since middle school, he'd been there for me through everything.

They started with her new movie and catching up on her life otherwise. She was so charming and personable, it was easy to see why everyone loved her. I'd experienced it firsthand, but just as a normal fan, it was hard to miss.

Then he put up a screenshot of the post she made about my most recent book, and I held my breath.

"You gotta breathe, babe," Aiden instructed, but I shushed him and waved my hand dramatically.

"So, when did you start reading Evin Morgan's books? Tell me the story."

And Lucy did. She talked about finding my first book in a little independent bookstore—making sure to mention the name of the store and compliment them on their wide selection—and how she was hooked immediately.

"I picked up the rest and then anxiously awaited each release from then on."

"And you mentioned it during one of your interviews about your upcoming movie?"

"Yeah, playing an author in the movie, I knew my favorite books were bound to come up. And it just so happens I had one of Evin's in my bag."

Simon smiled, and I knew what was coming. "Evin's, huh? So, you're on a first-name basis with her now, right?"

Lucy's face never faltered. She only smiled and looked out into the audience. "Why don't you just ask what you want to, Simon? You know you can shoot it straight with me."

"Of course. We've all seen the photos, Lucy. So, you went to Dallas yesterday to see Evin?"

"I did. I went to her signing, and we had dinner. But is that really what you want to know?"

Lucy winked at Simon, and the man actually blushed.

"She's good," Aiden whispered.

"When did your relationship start? You seemed awfully cozy. Was it before you began promoting her books?"

"There we go!" Lucy exclaimed, still completely unfazed. "The short answer is no, absolutely not. I pride myself on being a person of integrity, and that's not something I would ever do. Evin and I started messaging after I posted my review, and honestly, I fan-girled over her. I was surprised she didn't block me for all the stupid questions I asked about her writing."

I laughed quietly and chewed my thumbnail on my free hand. She had asked a lot of questions, but I loved every second of it.

"But the first time I saw her in person was yesterday during her book signing. I was at my family's house not too far away and made a quick stop. I couldn't pass up the opportunity to meet one of my favorite authors who just so happened to be one of my favorite people, too."

The smile she flashed the crowd was sincere, and they must have felt it, too, because everyone erupted in thunderous applause. Even Simon joined in, sitting back in his chair like a proud friend.

Once it finally died down, Lucy muttered a quick, "Thanks, guys," and turned back to the host.

"Okay, so nothing nefarious or insincere?"

"Oh, no. I'm honest, almost to a fault, and I wouldn't promote something that I didn't truly believe in. There were no ulterior motives here. I genuinely love her books."

Another round of applause and some of my anxiety ebbed.

"So, is this serious then? It looked pretty serious from those photos."

Lucy didn't miss a beat as she leaned forward. "Now, you know I can't spill *all* my secrets, Simon."

"Oh, come on, Lucy!" He exclaimed, getting the crowd in on it, too. I readjusted on the couch and tucked my legs against my chest.

Lucy shrugged and sipped her water, still cool and calm. She was made for this—the lights and attention. She was still the confident Lucy I knew, but I felt honored to know another side. The one few knew.

"As you know, a lot of my life is in the news, so sometimes it's nice to keep my private life private. At least for a while, but what I will say is that the past few months have been some of the best of my life."

More applause, and Aiden squeezed my hand. I chanced a quick glance his way and noted the knowing smile on his lips. I'd called him the moment I left Lucy's hotel room and spilled everything. Well, not *everything*. The more personal and intimate moments I'd kept to myself, but he'd known what happened.

"You look like a woman in love," Simon said off-handedly, and it was the first time I'd seen Lucy waver. She looked down at her hands folded in her lap, and I knew if she wasn't wearing makeup, we would've all seen her blush.

When she looked back up, her smile was back in place, although it was softer than before, like she was holding onto a secret. "I think anything more I should probably share with her first before I tell the world."

"Holy shit," Aiden muttered. "Lucy Lowe is in love with you."

Well, that makes two of us.

eighteen

. . .

Lucy

THE LAST FEW hours were long. I got off the stage and immediately set my plan in motion. After the required post-show meet-and-greet, more handshaking, and a *very* late dinner with Simon, it was almost two in the morning when I got back on the plane. I'd managed to send Evin a quick text between everything, but by the time I was able to call her, she didn't answer. It was three in the morning her time, so I assumed she was asleep.

Another long, three-hour flight was nothing when I knew I would see Evin on the other side. I tried to sleep on the plane, but I couldn't shut my mind off.

Once we landed, we went directly to her apartment, which was conveniently only fifteen minutes from the airport. But I spent those fifteen minutes trying to stop my spiraling thoughts. All I could think was, *this is why she shouldn't be with me.*

Being in the public eye, everything I did was primed for consumption. Privacy was often an illusion, and that was hard to live with.

I understood if she wanted to walk away. I would let her if

she wanted to. But if that were the case, I needed to see her at least one last time.

We pulled up at a little past six in the morning, which meant Evin had probably just woken up. I contemplated calling first before I knocked, but I was already standing in front of her door. With a shaking hand, I tapped on the wood and waited.

"Ms. Lowe, if she's not awake, we can come back," Derek whispered as an apartment door farther down the hallway opened. The woman stepped out, and her eyebrows shot to her hairline as she took in the four security people and me.

Recognition donned the moment the door in front of me opened.

It swung open, and the moment I saw Evin, a sense of calm washed over me. She was wearing a pair of slippers, pajama pants with little smiley faces all over them, and a black T-shirt. Her hair was in wild curls around her face, and her eyes were barely open.

She blinked warily and lowered her cup of coffee.

"Lucy?" she asked slowly. "Am I still dreaming, or are you really here?"

"I'm really here," I said, stepping inside and motioning to my security to stay put.

"Ms. Lowe, we really should—" Derek began, but the door was shut and locked before he could finish. I already knew what he was going to say—that they wanted to do a sweep of her apartment, but I was fine.

She walked farther into her apartment and set her coffee cup on her kitchen counter. I'd been intrigued and curious to know what Evin's apartment looked like. I'd seen it in the background of our video calls and photos, but I was much less concerned about it at that moment.

"I'm sorry I didn't call you back, but I finally fell asleep really late, and I just woke up." She yawned and turned back to me. My arms were around her in the next second.

She let out a surprised huff with the impact, but once she

steadied herself, she returned my embrace and buried her face in the side of my neck. I ran my fingers through her hair and down her back, pressing her tighter to me until there was no semblance of space left.

"What are you doing here?" she asked, pulling back and peering at me with tired hazel eyes.

"I couldn't wait to see you. After everything that happened, I just...I needed to see you."

"I'm okay, Lucy," she said. Her eyes swept over my face, and a soft smile tilted her lips. "Have you slept? You still have your makeup on, and I mean, your hair still looks great, too."

"No, I haven't slept. I finished with Simon and everyone else and immediately got on a plane. I'm so sorry that this happened," I said. My frustration and anger at that damn photographer for violating our privacy rose to the surface once again. I'd found a way to tamp it down during the interview and afterward, but now, looking at Evin, my heart hurt knowing she'd been hurt. "Fuck, Evin, I don't know what else to say besides I'm sorry."

"Hey, it's okay. And it's not your fault. I haven't blamed you for one second, babe. You didn't hire the photographer or leak the images. And the interview you did yesterday? It was amazing."

I took a deep breath and ran my hands down her sides. She shivered beneath my touch, and I dropped my hands, finally taking out the ponytail that had been giving me a brutal headache for the past several hours. I set the hair tie on her counter and ran my fingers through my hair. It probably looked insane, but the relief was instant.

"I didn't hire the photographer, but this is what it's like to be with me. Your life under the microscope and a headline at every turn."

When I looked back up at her, her arms were crossed over her chest, and she was shaking her head.

"I know," she said. I waited for her to continue, but she didn't.

"You know?"

She tossed her hands out to her sides in exasperation and walked farther into the kitchen. "Yes, I know. You made that clear last night, and I still decided to stay. And it's not like I wasn't aware of that before. You're everywhere, Lucy, and your previous relationships have been everywhere, too."

"Exactly, which is why I would understand if you didn't want anything to do with me. I can't guarantee this won't be the last time something like this happens."

A smile, one she was trying desperately to hide by rolling her lips and covering her mouth with her hand, still managed to slip into place.

Confused by her reaction, I didn't know what to do. I was so out of my depth. I felt at home in front of an audience or a camera. Working with the biggest names in the industry and meeting some of the most influential people in the world, I had no problem.

But standing in front of this gorgeous woman, hoping that she wouldn't walk away because of my life and my work, I was overcome with anxiety.

"Why are you smiling?"

"Because," she began, tugging her long sleeves down over her hands, "we're talking about the future when we haven't even discussed *now.*"

"Fuck, you're right," I sighed. We hadn't talked about anything beyond agreeing that we wanted to see one another again. But that was a problem I could easily solve.

Unsure what she would say, but knowing I had to try anyway, I crossed to her. My steps were slow, and she watched me, unmoving, with intent, curious eyes. I stopped directly in front of her and took a deep breath, which was an awful idea since all I could smell was her. The clean yet sweet jasmine scent scrambled my thoughts.

I reached out and brushed her hair over her shoulders before I cupped her cheeks.

"All I want is to be with you, Evin. And I really hope you want to be with me, too. I found the note you signed in my book, and I think it might be true. About our story."

Her smile was instant, and all my anxiety disappeared.

"I've already told you you're worth whatever may come, because I really want to be with you, too. And our story would be perfect. We just have to write it."

Unable to resist for another second, I slanted my mouth over hers, and my chest tightened the second I felt her lips against mine. She yielded to the kiss and relaxed into me, letting her hands fall to my hips. I slipped my tongue against the seam of her lips and moaned when she willingly opened for me. I savored the taste and feel of her tongue. I wanted to get lost in her again and again.

I wound my fingers in her hair and tugged her just the way I wanted. She did the same but stopped suddenly. Her lips froze, as did her hands in my hair.

"You have so much gel in your hair." She giggled against my lips. I pulled back and patted the top of my head. I hadn't even noticed before, but she was right. They'd used an absurd amount of product to keep my hair slicked back and my ponytail in place.

I cringed and untangled my fingers from my hair. Hours without sleep and going non-stop, I knew I looked a mess.

"No wonder my head itches."

Evin narrowed her eyes and laced her fingers through mine before she turned and started leading me across her apartment. We walked into her bedroom area that had the same exposed brick walls on the exterior and dark wood floors. Past her unmade bed with mustard sheets and fluffy pillows, she flipped on the light in her bathroom and pulled me inside.

She dropped my hand to pull the shower curtain back and turn on the water. For a studio apartment, the bathroom and shower were fairly spacious with white subway tiles throughout and a cute, patterned tile on the floor.

When she turned around, I was already tugging my shirt over my head and stepping out of my shoes. A shower sounded amazing.

"Are you getting in with me?"

She smiled and removed her shirt, exposing her perfect tits and stomach. She let her pajama pants slide down her legs, and just like that, she was naked while I was still struggling to tug off my jeans.

"Of course, I am," she said, pushing the curtain to the side. She stepped into the tub but glanced over her shoulder with a coy, tempting smile. "I wouldn't miss a chance to shower with my…*girlfriend.*"

She snapped the curtain shut, and I kicked my jeans to the side. When I stepped into the shower, she was already tipping her head back into the stream, water pouring over her face and slipping down her curves.

Dropping her chin, she pushed her hair back and smiled at me as she offered me her hand and tugged me under the water with her.

"Girlfriend," I murmured against her smiling lips. Water cascaded over us, and we finally stopped smiling long enough to taste each other. I wrapped my arms around her and pressed her wet body to mine. Her skin was already warmer from the water and felt perfect against me.

nineteen

. . .

Evin

I WAS SO glad she was there. After her interview, Aiden stayed over for a while until he eventually had to leave. I'd laid in bed scrolling through social media and news sites, reading the responses and hoping the tide would change in our favor, when I'd *finally* fallen asleep.

When my alarm went off at six that morning, I was exhausted, and my fingers immediately went for the snooze button. But the nerves crept back in the second I was conscious, and I had to get up, get a cup of coffee, and continue my diligent scroll through social media. And try to call Lucy.

But she showed up at my apartment, breathless and wearing the same makeup from the night before. She showed up, and she said all the things I'd wanted to hear, all the things I also wanted to say.

Now, I was standing in my shower with my girlfriend, the most beautiful and enigmatic woman on the planet.

"Girlfriend," she murmured, whispering against my lips. And I tried to stop smiling so I could kiss her correctly, but I was too happy.

I pressed my hands against her hips and spun her until she was beneath the water. Reaching up, I ran my fingers through her hair and did my best to wash the product out.

Lucy's eyes fell shut, and she dropped her head back. She held my waist, nails digging into my skin as her chest rose and fell with a long breath. Once her hair was drenched, I reached for the shampoo behind her and squeezed a healthy amount in my hand.

Her eyes dropped back down to mine as I tugged my fingers through her strands, and the excitement I saw behind the green morphed into a fiery desire that I could feel everywhere. She tightened her hold on me and held my stare as I washed her hair.

When it was properly lathered, I tilted her head back once again and let the water wash it away. We continued like that for a while. I helped Lucy wash her day away while our hands lingered and explored.

Steam circled around us, as did a heady desire. Lucy slammed her mouth down on mine and backed me into the cooler shower tile. I sucked in a sharp breath but all other thoughts disappeared when she lifted my right leg and placed my foot on the edge of the tub as she dropped to her knees in front of me.

"Lucy," I whispered as I ran my fingers through her hair.

"Yes?" she asked with a smile. "Unless you have something important to say, I would like to enjoy my girlfriend's cunt."

Efficiently silenced, I braced my free hand against the tile behind me and tried to stay standing as my knees weakened with the first firm swipe of her tongue. Her hands wrapped around me, gripping my ass and helping me stay standing.

She pressed my hips forward into her mouth, and my cries echoed through the bathroom over the pounding of water against the tile. Her skillful tongue lapped and kissed me, sweeping from my opening up to my clit where she pressed and sucked.

"That feels so good. You're just so good at this," I murmured, glancing down my body and watching her eyes flit up to meet mine. I could feel her smile against my skin, but she didn't stop.

She buried her mouth against me and fucked me with her tongue. Unable to stop myself, I ground myself against her, careful not to push too hard and knock her over. But Lucy had other ideas. Her fingers flexed against my ass as she urged me to move harder and faster.

Her tongue moved in and out of me, pushing in just far enough that I could clamp around it. My body begged for more, and she willingly gave it without a word from me. Especially since I was beyond words. The only things coming out of my mouth were pleading sounds, moans, and gasps that broke off when she did something new with her tongue.

My orgasm was swift and irresistible. It shot through me in one quick rush, overwhelming my senses and lingering beneath my skin long after it was over. I bucked and shook, but Lucy didn't stop. She held me steadfast against her mouth and let me ride out every wave of ecstasy.

Only when my pleasure-filled cries settled and my body stopped shaking with aftershocks did she stand and grace me with that perfect smile. I returned a sated one of my own as I turned off the water and reached behind her for one of the towels on the rack just outside the curtain.

I draped it over her shoulders and grabbed my own. We only took a few seconds to haphazardly dry off and stumble out of the shower before we were kissing and touching once again. Our arms wrapped around one another, I guided her into my room and onto my bed.

Her hands ran down my back as she parted her legs. Poised between them, I kissed her hard and deep.

"Wait," she mumbled against my lips, and I drew back to see her cringe and reach behind her. What she pulled out was the last thing I expected to see, and I was immediately mortified.

She held up my large wand vibrator and looked from it to me

and back again. A slow, tempting smile curved her lips, and it was almost like I could see all the dirty thoughts flitting behind her green eyes.

"And what is this doing in your bed?"

I knew Lucy wouldn't care, but it was my first reaction to lie about the real reason it was there. How I'd been unable to sleep after seeing her on the late show, and the only thing that helped my racing thoughts was the toy pressed between my legs and thoughts of her.

But I didn't lie—I licked my lips and tilted my head in consideration.

"I may have used it last night and fallen asleep before I could put it back in the drawer."

Her easy, seductive smile spread as she pressed the end of the toy against my chest. She hadn't even turned it on, but I shivered like I could feel the vibration when she brushed over my breast and my already peaked nipple.

She repeated the motion on the other side and continued down the center of my stomach as she asked, "And what were you thinking about when you were using it last night?"

"You," I breathed as my eyes slid shut.

"Details, baby. I need details."

Of course she did, but my brain was short-circuiting the closer she guided the toy to the aching spot between my thighs. I swallowed and forced my eyes back open, staring down at the gorgeous woman beneath me.

And I suddenly wanted to tell her all my dirtiest thoughts, all my unspoken fantasies, so we could experience them together.

With a stuttered breath, I licked my lips and tried to think straight.

"I was thinking about how hot you looked in that fucking suit with your ponytail and red lipstick. Then I imagined...I imagined you making me grind on your thigh again but while wearing that, and fuck, it was so hot."

Intrigue and desire sparked behind her eyes as her slow,

sensual smile slipped across her lips. The tip of the toy tapped against my clit, and I moaned as Lucy lunged forward and flipped us with ease. My back hit the sheets, and I gasped out a surprised laugh.

Her smile didn't falter as she leaned over me and placed a too-chaste kiss on my lips. I found myself chasing her mouth, eager for so much more, when she pulled back and settled between my legs.

"Well, I still have the suit, so next time, I'll put it on and let you grind against my lap until you leave a pretty little wet spot all over the expensive fabric."

"Fuck," I muttered under my breath. My head fell back onto the pillows behind me, and I was overwhelmed by the mental images her words spurred.

But I didn't have a spare moment to revel in them when the toy vibrated to life between my legs. My hips jolted off the bed, and I gripped the sheets beside me. The vibration, even on the lowest setting, ripped through me, shooting up my arms and down my legs.

My toes curled, and I looked down my body to see Lucy's gaze sweeping over me. She pressed the toy harder against me, and I groaned at the overwhelming, all-consuming sensation.

"*Lucyyyy*," I cried.

She pressed the button again, and the vibration increased. "Yes, scream my name, baby."

"This isn't fair," I ground out through clenched teeth, trying to stave off the orgasm for at least another few minutes.

She raised her dark eyebrows in silent question, and I reached for her hand covering the toy. "I'm not going to come again unless you do, too."

She held my stare for a moment and licked her lips as she swung her leg over one of mine and lined her pussy up with the toy. I couldn't contain the smile that slipped across my face as she lowered herself down. Her clit met the vibrating end of the wand, and her head tossed backward. She groaned toward the ceiling, and I pushed my hips up so the toy pressed harder against her.

I was rewarded with another sweet moan followed by a quick gasp as she looked back down at me. She met my thrust with one of her own, and my reaction was just as sudden and intense.

"Is this what you wanted?" she asked in a low, sultry voice.

I shook my head and gripped her thigh that was poised next to my hip. "It's better than anything I could have imagined. And I have a *really* good imagination."

We smiled at one another, but they quickly disappeared when she increased the vibration. Lucy ground down on the toy and pushed it harder against me. I did the same, pushing up against it, and we traded off like that for as long as we could hold out.

My nails dug into that perfect place where her hip curved, and I urged her to move faster and harder. With her free hand, she reached forward and kneaded my breast, pinching and pulling my nipple until the pleasure shot directly to my clit.

My entire body was alive under her touch and her gaze. I felt like I was floating on an electrified cloud, and I wanted to bottle the feeling for whenever I needed it. Except Lucy was mine, and I wouldn't need to bottle it. I could have it whenever I wanted it.

"You're so gorgeous," I murmured between moans. The early morning light peeking through my curtains shined across her skin and danced over her breasts. Her dark hair was slowly drying in perfect waves over her shoulders, and my hands itched to run my fingers through the strands.

But nothing held my attention like the vibration pinned between us and the orgasm that suddenly overwhelmed me. My entire body was overcome with unending pleasure.

"Fuck, fuck, *fuck*," I chanted as I held onto her tighter and clenched the sheets in my fist. "Lucy, oh my—"

My words cut off, and I forced my eyes to stay open so I

could commit to memory the twin ecstasy that tore across her face. Wave after wave of euphoria washed over us both.

"Yes, Evin. *Yes*," she chanted on a throaty moan. By the time we both came down, the vibrator was too much against my sensitive skin. She clicked it off and tossed the toy to the side as she dropped onto the bed next to me.

But I was still craving more of her. I tilted my head to the side and found her deep, green eyes staring back at me, the beginnings of a tired smile pulling at the corners of her mouth.

I pushed her unruly hair out of her face and brushed my hand down her back, tracing the dip of her spine and the curve of her ass.

"Two days ago, if you'd told me this would be my life, I never would've believed you. It feels like a dream."

I wasn't sure what I was saying, but it was harder *not* to spill my guts to the woman staring lovingly back at me.

"If this is a dream, I never want to wake up," Lucy whispered, and the happiness swelling in my chest bubbled up until I couldn't contain it, and a very girly giggle slipped free.

"Sorry," I said, covering my mouth with my hand and trying to stifle my laugh.

"It was a little cheesy," she admitted. She tugged my hand down, exposing my smile, and traced it with her thumb. "But you're just too sweet, Ev."

She rolled onto her side and wrapped her arms around me. I scooted closer until every part of us was touching, and my leg was pressed between hers. Her nose brushed against mine, and I took a deep breath, letting her sweet scent wash over me.

"Too sweet," she whispered. "And all mine."

epilogue

. . .

Lucy

Nine Months Later

THE POUNDING beat of the music vibrated through me as Evin led us through the crowd. Even wearing the bleach blonde wig—that made my head sweat like nobody's business—and sunglasses that looked ridiculous indoors, I was still worried that someone was going to recognize me.

But it was worth it to have a normal night out with Evin and her friends. Or at least as normal as it could be. We'd hung out with them so much at her apartment and at our new place, but it was something else entirely to be out with them.

Evin and I had spent the day doing all the things she'd once promised we would do. We went to every place we could on her never-ending list and had the best time. We kept as low of a profile as we could, and it had worked out as well as it could have.

This was after we'd spent the last week unpacking our new home. I'd sold my LA house quickly, and we'd bought something *much* smaller and more our vibe in the same neighborhood she'd lived in before.

It was perfect timing, too. I was between projects, and Evin was about to do her first book tour. A book tour she'd generously invited me on, and one in which I promised not to make about me. I was going to do whatever I had to to make it the best damn two weeks of her life.

We'd ended the day with dinner at her parents' house and made it home just in time to make it out with her friends. It was the perfect day. But then again, every day was perfect with Evin.

Evin held my hand as she led us toward the bar, but she still looked back, checking on me with an eager, excited smile. I returned it the best I could, even with the anxiety strumming through me, and gave her hand a quick squeeze.

Over the bobbing heads of the crowd, I saw Aiden's wide smile. Evin did a little happy wiggle when she spotted her best friend but didn't drop my hand as she hugged him and greeted everyone else.

"We're so happy you're here, Lucy!" Aiden yelled over the music and wrapped his arm around my shoulders. I hugged him back but cautiously looked over my shoulder, wanting to stay aware of my surroundings no matter how many security personnel were standing by.

Aiden noticed, though, and shifted us so my back was to the bar, and he was standing in front of me. He gave me a knowing smile and took our drink orders before waving down the bartender behind us.

Evin squeezed in next to me and slipped her hand around my waist, tugging me closer. I pushed my sunglasses on top of my head and glanced over at her. Her rich-brown hair was perfectly curled around her face, and her makeup made her eyes almost gold in the pulsing lights.

My eyes raked down her body, curves on display in her black top and matching leather skirt. Absolutely filthy thoughts—the same thoughts I'd had since she stepped out of our bedroom and asked for my opinion—filtered through my mind. There was nothing I could do to stop them, especially as she stood there, eyes darting from mine to my lips like she had all the same dirty thoughts.

Aiden handed us both our drinks, and we thanked him quickly, but our attention was immediately back on one another.

"You look like you're about to run," Evin said next to my ear, loud enough that I could hear her above the music.

I took a long sip of my drink and shook my head. "I would never run from you," I all but yelled back. She smiled but rolled her eyes at the same time, twisting her straw around in her tequila.

There was a challenge in her eyes when she looked back at me, and she lifted her drink to her lips, downing the rest of the nearly full glass in a few swallows. She set the glass down on the bar behind us and motioned to my still-full drink.

"Your turn?" she asked over the music. She motioned to my drink, and I gave her what I could only guess was a wide-eyed, surprised look. "I just want you to enjoy yourself, baby. So, finish your drink, and then we're going to dance."

It was my turn to roll my eyes, but I did as she suggested. I downed my drink and set my glass next to hers, squinting as the whiskey burned its way down my throat. I shook my head and waved at Evin to lead the way.

She took my hand, and we were once again weaving through the crowd of people. I could feel Aiden and a few of her other friends at my back and looked up to see one of my security staring directly at me from the edge of the dance floor.

Evin found the perfect place between people and spun to grace me with a smile I felt everywhere. Her hands tangled behind my head, running through the short strands of blonde hair as she tugged me closer.

My hands found her hips, and every part of me settled with her closeness. She dropped a kiss against my neck, and I tightened my hold on her. Her hips started moving to the music, and mine did the same. Feeling the music and letting the anxiety filter from my thoughts, I closed my eyes and positioned one of my legs between hers.

I felt her groan and smile against my neck just beneath my ear. My own satisfied smile slipped into place as we found the perfect rhythm. The rest of the world was miles away.

"I love you," I said, hopefully loud enough for her to hear me.

When she smiled at me, I knew she had. "I love you, too. So much." And my heart did that thing it always did when she said it. Where it felt like it might leap out of my chest.

"I like the blonde," she said, and I shook my head.

"I won't be going blonde permanently. It's only for tonight."

She pulled back and let her hands brush down the back of my neck. I shuddered at the sensation even as we kept dancing to the steady pounding rhythm.

"Yes, just for tonight. But you have to keep it on when we get home. I've never been with a blonde before."

I laughed and held her tighter.

Dropping my mouth to her ear, I said, "I can make that happen."

The music grew louder, and more people crowded onto the dance floor. But I barely noticed anyone else. I saw my security close by, and Aiden appeared next to us with a very large blond guy. The guy he'd just started seeing and whose name I couldn't remember with my perfect girlfriend in my arms.

That was as far as my attention traveled before Evin's fingers slipped up my neck and against the side of my face, urging me to look back at her and searing me with a panty-melting kiss when I finally did.

Soft lips, too sweet to be real, slipped against mine even as our bodies continued to writhe in time to the song. There were moments like these where it felt too good to be true. Where I needed to pinch myself to make sure it wasn't a dream.

That first night we'd finally met in person, after I'd admitted that I worried I'd never know real love, Evin said I'd know. And she was right.

I'd known then that I'd found the real thing. And I'm so glad I took a chance on it.

She was right about one more thing, too. Our love story was the greatest. We just had to keep writing it.

THE END

acknowledgments

I had the best time writing this book. Lucy and Evin were such vivid characters in my mind that they made it easy to write.

The entire idea for this story sparked from one photo. It was a photo of a celebrity holding a book in the airport, and I couldn't help but wonder what if that book was written by an indie author? How would that change their life?

Thus, Lucy and Evin were born.

Yes, this was my first WLW story, but it definitely won't be my last. I already have so many ideas! I just need the time to write them. And as a bisexual woman myself (woo, first time I've written that!), it was even more fun to explore their chemistry and story.

As always, thank you so much to my amazing alpha and beta readers. And to My Brother's Editor for making my words sparkle.

Mayhem Cover Creations never delivers a cover that is anything less than perfect. Like how pretty is this?!

And thank you to my amazing readers! Y'all are the best. Don't let anyone ever tell you any different.

also by grace turner

If you love this book, check out Grace Turner's other books. All available on Amazon and with Kindle Unlimited: https://amazon.com/author/graceturner

And to stay up to date on everything else Grace has to come, sign up for her newsletter at graceturnerauthor.com and make sure to check out:

instagram.com/graceturnerauthor

facebook.com/graceturnerauthor

tiktok.com/@graceturnerauthor

goodreads.com/graceturner

about the author

Grace Turner lives in Houston, Texas with her husband and two rambunctious pups and has a revolving door full of friends and family always visiting. By day, she works as a paralegal, and by night she reads, writes, and breathes contemporary romance

www.ingramcontent.com/pod-product-compliance
Lightning Source LLC
Chambersburg PA
CBHW052006220626
47052CB00004B/1117